Marjorie De

Josephine Chase

Alpha Editions

This edition published in 2022

ISBN : 9789356785878

Design and Setting By
Alpha Editions
www.alphaedis.com
Email - info@alphaedis.com

Contents

CHAPTER I.

MANAÑA

"Here I am—all booted and spurred and ready to ride," Marjorie Dean called out gaily to Veronica Lynne as Ronny entered the cool spacious patio of Lucero de la Manaña, the Lynnes' beautiful ranch home in southern California.

Marjorie was a feast for beauty-loving eyes as she sat on the wide stone edge of the silver-spraying fountain with its musical murmur of water splashing into a white marble basin. The mannish cut of her gray knickered riding clothes merely made her look more than ever like a little girl. From under her little round gray hat with its bit of irridescent color her bright brown curls showed in a soft fluff. She sat smiling at Ronny, a sleeve of her riding coat pushed back from one rounded arm, one hand trailing idly in the clear water of the basin.

"You *sound* like Paul Revere. At least, that is what he said, supposedly, on the night of his famous ride. You *look* like Leila Harper's friend, Beauty, even in riding togs." Ronny came over to Marjorie, smiling.

"I only remember Leila Harper." Marjorie glanced up teasingly.

"You are altogether too forgetful," Ronny lightly reproved.

She paused, looking amusedly down at her pretty chum. She was wearing a white linen, knickered riding suit which was vastly becoming. Her wide gray eyes gave out a happy light that her heart switched on every time her gaze came to rest upon Marjorie.

Since first she had known Marjorie Dean, back in their senior high school days at Sanford, she had cherished a pet dream. That dream had come true six weeks previous when Marjorie, her father and mother had arrived from the East to make Ronny a long deferred visit. To range the great ranch, pony-back, with Marjorie riding beside her, ever a gracious, inspiriting comrade, was Ronny's highest desire toward happiness.

"How long have you been waiting for me, Miss Paul Revere?" she playfully questioned. "Why didn't you come to Ronny's room and hang around? Why so unsociable?" Ronny drew down her face into an aggrieved expression which her dancing eyes contradicted. "I've known you to be much more cordial at old Wayland Hall."

"Oh, I've only been here about three minutes. I'm miles more sociable than I was at Wayland Hall," laughed Marjorie. "I thought you'd be ready and ahead of me. When I found you weren't, I couldn't resist stopping to dabble my hand in the water. I love the patio, Ronny, and adore the fountain. If I lived here three months longer I should be so steeped in the beauty of Manaña that I'd forget the East—maybe." Her "maybe" was stronger than her light prediction.

"The magic spell of Manaña is upon you," Ronny confidently asserted. "There is a mystical, romantic beauty about Manaña. I have searched for it over and over again in the East, but have never found it. It seems to me our Manaña is Nature's own ideal of grandeur and beauty. I think the Spanish influence in the house and about the ranch heightens its claim to the romantic. Hamilton Arms has a certain stateliness of beauty, all its own. But has it anything more romantically beautiful than this patio?"

"It's true as you live, Ronny Lynne," agreed Marjorie gaily.

"You couldn't love the patio better than I do." Ronny cast a fond glance about the great square-covered court with its central crystal-spraying fountain and its ancient stone floor, gay with rugs and colorful Navajo blankets. The few inviting lounging chairs, the reading stand piled with current magazines, the quaint leather-covered Spanish couch, long and narrow, and heaped with gorgeous-hued silken cushions seemed only to accentuate the primitive charm of the old-time inclosure. Above it a railed-in Spanish balcony extended around the four sides. It was bright with flowering plants and further beautified by the masses of trailing vines which clambered over the old-time mahogany railing.

"I know it." Marjorie gave a quick nod. "I'd not wish to love it as much as Hamilton Arms. I never thought I could care more for the Arms than dear Castle Dean. But I do. My whole heart is bound up in it, and Hamilton. I hope that I—that—we—will—" Marjorie stopped, her color deepening. "I hope Hal and I will live at Hamilton some day." She continued in shy haste to finish what she had begun to say when girlish embarrassment had overtaken her.

"I believe Hamilton to be the one place for you and Hal to live," Ronny made hearty response. "It would be splendid if General and Captain should decide to live in Hamilton Estates, too. 'Where the treasure is, there shall the heart be also,' you know. You are General's and Captain's treasure, and Hamilton is your treasure, so why shouldn't you all get together and be happy? None of you have really anything special to bind you to Sanford. That is, not as you have at Hamilton." Ronny smiled very tenderly at Marjorie's glowing face.

"It's different with me," Ronny continued. "My treasure is Father. So Manaña means most of any place on earth to me. I love Hamilton devotedly. Remember, there are plenty of Travelers to help complete the dormitory, but only one Traveler to comfort a lonely man. Father has considered me above himself always. Now I must begin to consider him."

Marjorie sprang up from her seat upon the fountain's stone edge. "It's odd to me still, Ronny—being engaged to be married to Hal," she confessed as she shyly busied herself with the drying of her wet hand with her handkerchief.

Ronny nodded sympathetically. "I always believed it would happen some day," she said. "You can't help but feel strange about it, though. You've hardly seen him since college closed."

"But I'm going to see him soon." The note of unmistakable happiness in Marjorie's reply was in itself convincing of the true state of the little Lieutenant's heart.

The two friends had now passed through the arched stone doorway of the patio and stepped out upon the lawn. They crossed it to the ancient brick drive and followed the drive toward a point near the heavy iron entrance gates, where a young Mexican boy stood holding the bridles of two horses. The girls were going for a ride before sunset.

"*Bueno; muy bueno, Ramon. Muchas gracias* (Good; very good, Ramon. Thank you very much)," Ronny brightly smiled her further thanks at the pleased groom.

Ramon showed white teeth, acknowledging her thanks in Spanish. Due to her love of action Marjorie had learned to ride with a readiness which delighted and amazed Ronny. She had picked for Marjorie a handsome white pony which she had fancifully named Dawn. Pony and rider had quickly become fast friends. Ronny's own pet mount, Lightning, a soft black thoroughbred that deserved his name, was the admiration and the despair of the majority of the cowboys on the ranch. Few besides Ronny and Mr. Lynne had been able to stay long upon his back. He obeyed Ronny because he loved her.

"Your going home will leave a horrible blank space at my hearthstone," Ronny regretfully told Marjorie as they rode their ponies slowly through the opened gates and out onto a broad trail which descended gradually in an easterly direction.

"I wish you could be in two places at once," Marjorie returned with a soft little sigh. "I hate to leave you, Ronny. What are we going to do without you on the campus? What are Page and Dean without their greatest show feature? Think of all you've done as a Traveler for the good of Hamilton. I haven't dared write Miss Susanna and the girls that you weren't coming back. Does your father know yet what good fortune's in store for him?"

"No; I've not broached the subject to him yet. Before long he will probably ask me when I think of going East. Then I shall say 'Not at all,' and stick to it."

"You'll simply *have* to come East to—to—" She paused, her eyes meeting Ronny's with a significantly happy light.

"Oh, of course, *then*," Ronny smilingly emphasized.

"You are to be one of my bridesmaids, Ronny," Marjorie decreed. "I've been thinking quite a lot about my wedding. I have an idea that it will be different from most weddings, I'd like to have gathered around me that day the girls I've known and loved best. I'm going to try to find a place for them all in my bridal procession. I've not settled upon a single thing yet, but I have just one inspiration that I hope I can carry out."

"When is it to be, Marjorie?" Ronny questioned with the lighting of her fair face which Marjorie loved to see.

"I don't quite know yet. It will all depend on when the dormitory is finished. I—I haven't made any plans for it except I've thought to myself about the kind of wedding I'd like to have. I've said more to you than I have even to Captain," Marjorie declared with a shy laugh.

"I am highly honored, Marvelous Manager." Ronny leaned to the right in her saddle with a respectful bow. "Having marvelously managed everything and everybody for a period of years on the campus, may we not expect you to manage your own wedding with *eclat*?"

"Don't expect too much," Marjorie warned laughingly.

As they talked the ponies had been impatiently enduring the slow walk to which their riders, absorbed in confidences, had put them. The trail was broad and smooth; wide enough for two ponies to run on, side by side. It dipped gradually down into a green valley of oak, larch and aspen trees. There the trail narrowed to a bridle path, winding in and out among wooded growths, and overhanging steep ravines. After half a mile it emerged from shadowed woods into the sunshine of the open country, growing wider again.

"There he is!" Ronny had been keeping up a bright look-out ahead. Her white-clad arm began a vigorous signaling to a horseman who had reined in near a large rock some distance ahead of them. He was sitting on a big bay horse, waiting for the riders to come up.

Every day, since Marjorie had learned to ride the two girls had gone pony-back at sunset to meet Mr. Lynne on his return from the daily supervision of the planting of a peach orchard of choice variety.

"I'll race you," Ronny challenged. She started her horse, Lightning, with a quick pat of her hand on his silky neck. He shot forward like a veritable streak of lightning, glad of a chance to run.

CHAPTER II.

FOND REALITY

Dawn was only a second or two behind him. The pair of mettlesome ponies fled along the trail toward the waiting horseman, their riders uttering buoyant little cries of encouragement and laughter. It was the usual race, and Ronny always won. Dawn could not quite keep up with Lightning.

"*Buenos dias, señor* (how are you, sir)?" Ronny greeted cheerily as she reined in near her father's horse. "Stand and deliver. What's in that fat, interesting package at your saddle bow? I can guess. You've been to Teresa's."

"Who is Teresa?" Mr. Lynne inquired with guileless interest.

"Teresa is a most amiable Spanish donna who is famed for the deliciousness of her candied fruits, such as you have in two tin boxes wrapped in one package," Ronny triumphantly informed. "Get down from your horse, Señor Lynne, and hand over the spoils to us. If you're good, we may ask you to sit beside us on that nice flat rock over there and attend a picnic."

"You win. Come and get it." Mr. Lynne had sprung from his horse and was waving the large package temptingly at Ronny. Marjorie sat on her pony, watching the devoted pair with an affectionate smile. She was thinking that Mr. Lynne was almost as dear and full of fun as General. But not quite, she made loyal reservation.

Ronny had left Lightning's back in a twinkling and was making energetic grabs at the package her father was swaying back and forth just out of her reach.

"You're in this, Lightning. Candy, old dear. Think of that." The pony sent up an approving whinny. Dawn also began to neigh vigorously. "Can't fool you two beauties. You know what's in those boxes as well as I."

Ronny managed to secure the package. She had the wrapper off of it in a flash, revealing two square tin boxes such as she was famed for having provided at the Travelers' campus spreads. She handed one of the tin boxes to Marjorie and sat down on the flat rock with the other on her lap to explore its contents.

"Um-m. Cherries, apricots and plums!" she exclaimed. "Two hours yet till dinner. Sit down, Señor Lynne and Señorita Dean. You're invited to a feast."

"Teresa sends you her best wishes and says she will have plenty of candied fruit packed for you by the time you are ready to go East to Hamilton."

Teresa was the wife of Mr. Lynne's oldest foreman and was noted for her skill in candying fruit.

"Teresa doesn't know yet that I'm not going East again this fall." Ronny turned calm gray eyes upon her father as she bit into a luscious cherry.

"I'm afraid you will have to go," Mr. Lynne said with apparent regretful seriousness. He was a big fair giant of a man with penetrating blue eyes, a strong square chin and thick fair hair brushed high off his broad forehead. His facial expression was kindly, yet suggested great will-power.

"I am going to Mexico on a prospecting trip for silver. I promised some friends of mine long ago that I would join their expedition. I shall be gone all winter. I can't take you with me, and I don't wish you to be alone at Manaña. It's lucky I can pack you off to Hamilton again. Such a strain off my mind," he ended teasingly.

"You are a sham," Ronny set the box of cherries on the ground. Her arms went round her father's neck. She placed a playful hand to his lips. "Not another word. You know you only think I want to go East again. So you have joined——"

"Well, don't you?" her father tenderly demanded.

"Not more than to stay here with you," she answered honestly.

"But how can you stay here with me when I shan't be here? You aren't going to say I can't go to Mexico, are you?" he put on an expression of blank disappointment.

"Can you say on your word of honor that you aren't going away on my account?" Ronny countered severely.

"You haven't answered my questions yet," came the laughing evasion. "Besides you took me so by surprise that I forgot I had two letters for Marjorie."

Mr. Lynne reached into a pocket of his tweed riding coat and drew forth two envelopes. One was square and pale gray. The other was square and white. Sight of it sent two happy color signals flying to Marjorie's cheeks. Hal's familiar hand on the white square made her heart beat faster. Quickly she laid the gray envelope over it, striving to keep her lovely face from indexing her love for Hal. She bent purposely wrinkled brows over the gray envelope. It bore a San Francisco postmark. The writing on it seemed oddly familiar, yet she could not place it. So far as she knew she had neither acquaintances nor friends in San Francisco. She courteously tucked both letters into a coat pocket and again turned her attention to the merry little tilt still going on between Ronny and her father.

"I'll confess, if you will," Mr. Lynne was saying. "But you first."

"Confess what?" Ronny put on a non-comprehending air.

"Can you truthfully say that you'd rather stay at home this year than go back to Hamilton and finish your part of the work of building the dormitory?" There was an undercurrent of seriousness in the light tone of the question.

"When you put matters that way, no. You're awfully mean." Ronny laughed half vexedly. "Now it's my turn. Hadn't your friends forgotten all about that silver expedition until you reminded them of it? Why need you go prospecting when you are not a prospector?"

"I really don't know much about my friends' memories. I am obliged to become a prospector in order to make you go back to Hamilton. It's the only way. Now, isn't it?"

"I can't think of any other," Ronny admitted. "It's dear in you." There was a tiny quaver in her clear enunciation.

"Not a bit of it. It's necessary for you to return to Hamilton to finish your part of the dormitory enterprise," came her father's crisp decision. "Never undertake a thing unless you are prepared to finish it, Little Comrade." It was her father's pet name for Ronny. "What do you say, Marjorie?" he turned to the radiant-faced Lieutenant.

"I ought to be sympathizing with you because you won't see Ronny this winter. But if you only knew how we need her on the campus. She is Page and Dean's greatest show feature, not to mention what she is to the Travelers and the dormitory enterprise. It's the best news I could possibly hear," Marjorie said with happy enthusiasm.

Seated on the flat rock and enjoying Teresa's delicious candied fruit an hour winged away before the trio ended their absorbed confab and rose to take the trail to Manaña. The sun was fast dropping in the West, a huge flaming ball against the pale tints of the evening sky.

Mounted again upon Dawn's back Marjorie gazed dreamily across the broad acres of Manaña. The great ranch lay in waves of undulating green forest and meadow, rising in the east to distant purple-tipped heights. She was experiencing an odd sense of unreality in the scene. Was it really, she, Marjorie Dean, who looked down from a height upon a magnificent verdant summer world so far removed from the one she had ever known. To her, Lucero de la Manaña was indeed the star of the morning—but of a magic realm.

Reality? Her hand sought the pocket of her riding coat in which reposed Hal's letter. She had told Ronny that it seemed strange to her to be betrothed to Hal. Her fingers closed around the envelope that held his letter with the conviction that, after all, Hal was the beloved reality; Manaña was a beautiful illusion.

She knew in her glad heart that she had not dreamed of a spring night of magic and moonshine when she had walked with Hal in the sweet fragrance of Spring, aflower, and felt the tender clasp of his arms and the touch of his lips on her own. She had not dreamed that she had promised him her future when her work should have been done. It was all true.

CHAPTER III.

THE ROAD TO THE HEART'S DESIRE

Marjorie rode back to the ranch house in a kind of tender daze. She heard Ronny's and Mr. Lynne's voices addressing her, and her own voice answering them as far-off sounds. For one who had formerly never understood love she could not but marvel at the great change within herself. She was now experiencing the stillness of happiness of which Constance had tried to tell her when she had confided to Marjorie the news of her engagement to Lawrence Armitage. Constance had said then she hoped Marjorie would some day fall in love with Hal. Marjorie smiled as she recalled the half displeased reply she had made. How hard-hearted she had been. She was remorseful now. Loving Hal with all the strength of her fine nature she could not forgive herself for having caused him so much of lover's pain.

Alone in her high-ceilinged, luxurious sleeping room at the ranch house she dropped hastily into a wicker arm chair and drew the cherished letter from her pocket. Her smile was a thing of tender beauty as she opened the envelope and extracted two closely written sheets of thick gray paper. Hal's letters to Marjorie had usually been brief affairs until after the eventful spring evening when she had turned life from drab to rose for him. Love had given his pen new impetus. With starry eyes and heightened color Marjorie read his fond salutation:

> "Dearest:
>
> "Your latest letter told me the news I have been waiting anxiously for. You are coming home soon. So glad you and General and Captain expect to be at Severn Beach by the twelfth of September. Connie and Laurie arrived here from New York last week. You must have heard from Connie by now. I am planning a moonlight stroll on the beach and a sail in the Oriole for the same old six of us who went strolling and sailing on a certain white moonlight night last summer; the unhappiest I have ever known. So I am sure that our next stroll together in the moonlight will be the happiest.
>
> "It is such a long way to Manaña. I have to remind myself often that the violet girl who made me a wonderful promise one night at Hamilton Arms was real, and not a dream. I shall not be sure of my good fortune until we meet again. You went away from me to Ronny's so soon after that enchanted night. I had not had time to realize my great happiness. How came

> you to love me, I am always wondering, when there seemed no hope? You will tell me how it came to pass. Won't you, sweetheart?
>
> "There is so much I should like to say to you. I cannot write it. Whenever I try to write you my whole thought is that I love you and hope soon to see you."

Marjorie read on, the starriness on her brown eyes softening to wistful tenderness. The depth of Hal's love for her filled her with a strange tender humility. She could hardly believe herself worthy of such devotion.

She sat immersed in her love dream until the tinkling chime of the French clock on the mantel shattered it.

"*Seven*," she counted in consternation, sentiment fading to dismay. "And I've not started to change my riding togs yet. I'll surely have to hurry."

Half past seven was the dinner hour at Manaña. Marjorie dropped a light kiss upon Hal's letter and hurriedly deposited it in a drawer of the dressing table. She plumped down on a cushioned stool and began a quick removing of her riding boots. By twenty minutes after seven she was deftly hooking her slim form into a sleeveless white faille frock, charmingly embroidered with little clusters of rosy double daisies. It had been a present to her from Leila who was abroad with Vera, and had come from "L'harmonie" the most exclusive shop in Paris. Marjorie, full of devotion toward Hal, had picked out the gown to wear down to dinner as somehow expressing her best in her happiness.

"Five minutes to spare." She closed the last snap with satisfaction. "I could do my hair a little smoother, but it's pretty fair, Bean, pretty fair." She said this last aloud, laughing a little. It brought pleasant memories of Jerry Macy.

She reopened the drawer, holding Hal's letter with intent to read it again. Then she remembered the other letter in the pocket of her riding coat and went smiling into the small adjoining dressing room for it. She was chipping open an end of its envelope when Ronny knocked on the door.

"Come," Marjorie called.

Ronny opened the door and entered, her individually charming self in a crystal-beaded white frock of chiffon.

"I forgot all about this letter." Marjorie held up the square envelope. "I—you see—the other was from Hal, and——"

"I understand perfectly." Mischief gleamed in Ronny's gray eyes. The two girls laughed. "Go ahead and read the one Hal didn't write. I give you permission. Three minutes yet until the dinner ring."

"Thank you, kind Ronny." Marjorie made Ronny a gay little obeisance. "I haven't the least idea who it's from." Marjorie now had the letter out of the envelope and was searching it for the signature. She found it, stared at it in surprise, then cried: "This letter is from Leslie Cairns. Pardon me while I read it." A moment or two and she dropped into a chair, glancing up at Ronny rather helplessly.

"Why, she has written the *last* thing I'd expect her to write!" she exclaimed wonderingly.

"Leslie Cairns always was a surprising person," Ronny remarked with good-humored satire. "Only her surprises were generally more startling than agreeable."

"I am sure she wouldn't mind if I read you her letter. Wen Lo hasn't rung the bell yet. We still have a minute." Marjorie commenced in a brisk tone:

> "DEAR MISS DEAN:
>
> "My father and I lunched at the Arms with Miss Hamilton several weeks ago and from her learned that you were visiting Miss Lynne in California, at Lucero de la Manaña.
>
> "We came West over a week ago on a flying business trip. My father is trying to initiate me into the mysteries of financiering. I find them decidedly intricate. We are now in San Francisco, and staying at the Albemarle. Our telephone number is Oakland 842. If you should come to San Francisco in the near future will you not look me up?
>
> "My real reason for writing, however, is this. We shall go East before long in my father's private car, the Speedwell. Can your father and mother and you not arrange to be our guests on the eastern journey? We shall be glad to suit our time for going East to your own. It would be a great pleasure for my father and me to meet your father and mother, and entertain them and you. We are both ambitious to serve the interests of Hamilton. We feel, that, aside from the pleasure of yours and your parents' company, you will be able to teach us the way to be of use to Hamilton College. We shall be in the neighborhood of the Lynne ranch next Tuesday and will stop for a few moments to see you. Think the matter over and be prepared to say 'yes.'

"Cordially yours,

"LESLIE A. CAIRNS."

"And Leslie Cairns wrote that letter!" Ronny made a gesture of incredulity. "It seems hard to believe she isn't Jeremiah's Hob-goblin any longer."

"It seemed queer to me for a little while last June to think of her as a friend," Marjorie confessed. "That feeling soon died out of my mind. After she took the stand she did about the Leila Harper Playhouse I had a great deal of admiration for her. I knew she was truly sincere in her resolve to be different."

Marjorie referred to a certain decision at which Leslie had arrived after she had visited Hamilton Arms in company with her father one day during the previous spring. It was then Leslie had outlined to Marjorie her generous proposal to erect a theatre on the site of her garage "flivver" which she wished to name "The Leila Harper Playhouse." The theatre was to be owned and controlled by Leila with only the one stipulation that whatever performances might be given in it should be for the benefit of the Brooke Hamilton Dormitory.

Marjorie had then urged Leslie to permit her name to be given as the donor of the theatre when it should be completed the following spring. Leslie had confided to Marjorie her great desire that her father should be named as the giver of the theatre. Her own unworthy record at Hamilton College forbade her that pleasure. She had somberly argued that mention of either her name or her father's as the giver of the theatre would serve only to recall her misdeeds and expulsion from Hamilton to faculty and students alike. She had already disappointed her father too greatly, she told Marjorie, without placing either him or herself in line for further criticism.

"I'm going to tell you something, Ronny. Leslie gave me permission last spring to use my own discretion in regard to keeping it a secret. Miss Susanna and Jerry know. So does Robin. I'd rather the other girls shouldn't for awhile. You see it's something wonderful for Leila. We wish it to be a great surprise. She's so quick to divine things. I'm awfully afraid she may find it out unless I am very careful." Marjorie put Ronny in possession of Leslie's pet plan.

"There ought to be some way, Ronny, to manage things so that Leslie or her father—she'd rather it would be he—might be named as the giver of the Leila Harper Playhouse at the dedication and presentation." Marjorie laid Leslie's letter on the willow magazine stand with a little sigh.

"There will be." Ronny made the assertion with positiveness. "What a splendid thing for Leslie Cairns to wish to do! The way will open for her. You'll see. She is trying earnestly to think of everyone but herself. And that is truly the only sure road to the heart's desire."

CHAPTER IV.

A TWILIGHT SERENADE

After dinner that night in the beautiful summer dining room which opened upon a broad side veranda, tropically picturesque with palms and oleanders, Marjorie and Ronny repaired to their favorite haunt. It was a second-story balcony which overlooked a rose garden. There Wen Lo, the enigmatic-faced Chinese butler, long in the service of the Lynnes, brought them their dessert of ices and sweets and coffee. Mr. Lynne had declined dessert and gone into the library to enjoy an after-dinner cigar and a new book on fruit culture which had been written by his Chinese friend and ranch neighbor, Sieguf Tah.

"You must be feeling both glad and sorry about going back to Hamilton, Ronny," Marjorie said presently drawing in a deep breath of the fragrant, rose-scented air. "Glad to be at Hamilton, and with us; sorry to leave Manaña. It's so beautiful at all times. One day I think I love the early mornings best. Next day, it's the sunset that seems most beautiful. Now the twilight's coming on, and the roses are so sweet. Oh-h-h!"

A sturdy trellised vine, odorous with scented clusters of pinkish-yellow roses clambered up and over the balcony. Marjorie bent and buried her face in the clustered riot of bloom.

"You've learned, even in this short time, to love Manaña in the way I love it," Ronny said softly.

A pleasant silence ensued between the two friends, Ronny, gazing absently into the approaching twilight, seemed lost in reverie. Her finely-chiseled profile turned toward Marjorie gave her the look of a young Greek goddess, dispassionately viewing a world of her own ruling.

As the twilight merged into dusk and the first stars of evening lit their twinkling lamps, from underneath the balcony the musical beat of a guitar rose in rhythmic measure. Came a characteristic Spanish prelude, then an old Mexican love song floated out upon the rose-scented dusk, sung by a trio of golden-voiced Mexican boys.

"*La serenata* (the serenade)," Ronny murmured, "How dear in Father. He has asked Teresa's sons to serenade us. They are singing a very old Mexican song called, '*Mi novia.*' That means 'my sweetheart.'"

Ronny became silent again with this brief explanation. The dulcet, mellow voices of the Mexican boys swelled enchantingly upon the stillness of the evening. Marjorie was sure she had never before listened to anything more tenderly romantic than the plaintive rise and fall of the old song. More than once she had heard from Ronny of the fine singing voices which were the natural heritage of the Spanish Mexicans.

The singers followed their tuneful offering with another old Spanish ballad which Ronny told Marjorie was called "The Love Tears."

"Cuando de tu lado ausente,

Triste muy triste es mi vida!"

rose the high sweet tenor of Ricardo, Teresa's oldest son.

"When thou art absent from my side,

Sad, how sad, is my life!"

Ricardo was eighteen and still heart-whole yet the Latin inheritance of heartbreak was in his voice. All the sadness of an unrequited love, which he had certainly never yet experienced, rang in his impassioned singing. Nor were the voices of his younger brothers scarcely less emotional. The wistful yearning golden notes were no more than the heritage of romance and sentiment so peculiarly Spanish.

When the song was done Ronny leaned over the balcony and called softly down to them in Spanish: "*Hermosa* (beautiful). *Que se repetia* (please sing again). *Muy bien venido, amigos. Nos alegramos mucho de que nos honre con su compania.* (Welcome, friends. We are glad of the honor of your company.)"

The serenaders had been standing well under the overhanging balcony. Now they stepped out from its shadow a little, three dark outlines in the paler dusk.

"*Muchas gracias, Señorita Veronica* (thank you, Miss Veronica)." came the full-toned voice of Ricardo in pleased return. He went on to say in English. "Señor Lynne, your father, has asked us to give you the serenade on our way to the *fiesta* this evening which is to be at Pedro's house in honor of his birthday. We are pleased to sing for you and the señorita from the East. Now we will sing for you your favorite song, '*Pregunte las estrelles.*' Then we must hurry or be late to sing the birthday song for Pedro."

"*Muchas gracias*, Ricardo. Señorita Dean and I love your songs. Presently we shall walk over to Pedro's *casa* (house) to look in upon the *fiesta*. We have been invited by Annunciata, his wife. Tomorrow evening I wish you to bring Donna Teresa with your brothers to a *fiesta* here. The mother and father of Señorita Dean will then be there. They will wish to hear you sing."

Followed a quick flow of appreciative Spanish, then a pair of musicianly hands picked out a ravishing little prelude on the guitar. Again the three in the soft darkness below took up the heart-stirring, painful sweetness of one of the old-time Spanish *cantares* (songs).

"Perhaps the stars in Heaven

Know this night how much I love:"

Marjorie had learned a few Spanish words since she had come to Manaña. She could not understand those of the song. Nevertheless she understood its import. Ronny had translated the title for her. She was now lost in happy wonderment as to whether the stars in Heaven could possibly know how truly she loved Hal.

With the ending of the song she called down pleasantly to the three young men. "Thank you for your beautiful singing. I think 'The Stars' is the sweetest song you sang."

"We are happy to have pleased you, *hermosa* (beautiful) señorita. It is the song we also like best." Ricardo added something daringly respectful to Ronny in Spanish. She laughingly translated his speech as the three dark figures strode away across the lawn. "Ricardo says that you are the most beautiful young lady he has ever seen."

"Oh, bother." Marjorie's tone was half vexed. "I wish I had a pug nose and freckles. No. I'm glad I haven't them." She turned the subject abruptly with: "I should not have understood the beauty of those songs last year as I do now. Love has opened a new, wonderful world to me."

"And this is hard-hearted Marjorie Dean to whom I'm listening," Ronny said in a tone of light incredulity. Candidly she added: "I know how you feel about love. I feel so about it now. I see nothing deeper in Ricardo's songs than beauty of voice and unconscious expression. Teresa says Ricardo has never been in love. His brothers are young boys of only twelve and fourteen. But the Spanish Mexicans have emotion in their voices when they are mere babies."

"Have you ever known a young man you thought you cared a little for?" Marjorie asked half curiously. She could not recall in her several years of friendship with Ronny that her brilliant talented friend had ever accorded more than careless attention to a young man of her acquaintance.

"No, I have not, and I don't wish to," Ronny replied with considerable emphasis. "I never expect to meet any such person. I couldn't fall in love if I tried."

"That's what I used to think." Marjorie held up a warning hand. "Be careful," she continued, laughing softly. "The moment when you are the most certain that you can *never* fall in love may be the signal for a change in your destiny. You may never *fall* in love. You may just *tumble* into it someday without a sign or word of warning."

CHAPTER V.

ON THE SPEEDWELL

"I've always tried my hardest to get whatever I wanted for myself no matter how much trouble I made for other people in the getting. Now here I am, caught in a snare. What's hardest of all to bear, Marjorie, is having hurt Peter the Great. Because I behaved like a vandal at Hamilton he's ashamed in his heart to come back to Carden Hedge to live the year round."

Seated opposite Marjorie on the comfortable observation platform of Peter Cairns' luxurious private car "Speedwell," Leslie cast a gloomy glance at her pretty companion out of remorseful eyes.

"That's why I realized what a mistake it would be to have that Leila Harper Playhouse business announced in chapel with my father's and my name attached," Leslie continued. "Again if it were announced in chapel with us left out it might start a whole lot of wondering about whom I had sold the garage site to, et cetera. Every move Peter and I made afterward would be watched. Of course we'd be found out. Then someone might start a rumor that we were ashamed to come forward because of my misdeeds. It would be true, but not very pleasant. If we wait till the theatre is built and ready for Leila we'll have a good chance of getting away with it, sub rosa."

"I like the idea of waiting until the theatre is finished before honoring Leila in chapel," Marjorie returned frankly. "But, Leslie, by then you may feel differently about not wishing your name or your father's given."

"No; I shan't. I'm very sure I shan't." Leslie moodily shook her head. "It can never be that way, Marjorie. I wish it could."

It was the last afternoon of the journey across continent which Mr. and Mrs. Dean and Marjorie were completing in Peter Cairns' private car. The next morning would see the travelers in New York City. From New York the Deans were going for two weeks to their favorite summer resort, Severn Beach.

Marjorie had not altogether relished the idea of the journey East in so much exclusive luxury. She had looked forward to the merry more democratic canopy of the Pullman car where from San Francisco to Chicago they might count upon finding plenty of pleasant traveling acquaintances in the same car with themselves. They had had great fun going West.

Yet it had seemed to her that an acceptance of Leslie's invitation was the only true way of showing Peter Cairns' daughter that she held nothing of the past against her. Leslie and her father motored to Manaña there to extend their invitation to the Deans in person. Marjorie's General and Captain had left the decision to her.

During the enjoyable trip East Leslie and Marjorie had had time to grow gradually acquainted with each other in a pleasant, half reserved fashion which promised someday to merge into a real friendship. Thrown in each other's company the two girls had discussed little else except the subject of Hamilton College. Leslie was never tired of hearing of the funny sayings and doings of Leila, Jerry and Muriel Harding. She discussed her own troubles with the San Soucians as their ring-leader in a humorous fashion which Marjorie found vastly amusing. It had revealed in Leslie a keen sense of humor which Marjorie had often suspected her of possessing even in her lawless days.

While she talked freely of Hamilton College as she had known it when a student there Leslie had thus far pointedly avoided mention of the one thing she wished most to tell Marjorie. She and Marjorie had more than once discussed her determination to present Leila with the directorship of the theatre anonymously when the playhouse should be completed. Under the able management of Peter Graham work on the new theatre had been going forward steadily since the previous June.

On this last afternoon of the journey Mr. and Mrs. Dean, Peter Cairns and his confidential secretary, Wilkins, were deep in a game of whist in the small salon of the Speedwell. Marjorie and Leslie had the observation platform to themselves. Soberly glancing at Leslie's clouded features Marjorie felt nothing but the deepest sympathy for the girl she had once been tempted to rank as an enemy. She was understanding only too clearly the difficulties which now beset Leslie's proposed path of benevolence.

"Never is such a long time, Leslie," Marjorie's tone was brightly comforting. "It's two years, you know, since you left college. Most of the students you knew then, or who knew of you, have been graduated. There is a much better spirit abroad on the campus, too, than in the old days." Marjorie stopped, flushing. "I didn't mean to remind you—" she began contritely.

"No harm done, Bean." A faint lighting of Leslie's dark features accompanied the ridiculous nickname she had once derisively given Marjorie. "Of course there's a better spirit now on the campus. You won what you fought for. But there are a certain number of students there still who would love to pick me to pieces, given an opportunity. It would be said of me that I was trying to make money cover my flivvers."

"But your motive is sincere," Marjorie cried. "Besides the theatre is not to be built on the campus. I think you ought to brave matters out, Leslie. The

Travelers will stand by you through thick and thin. We understand how generous you are, and in time we shall make others see it. That is, if there should be others. Sometimes one sweeping act of nobility such as you propose to do changes everything for the best."

"It won't for me," was Leslie's pessimistic prediction. "It's not really about myself I care. To honor Leila, and help the dorms along. What more can one ask?" Leslie made an earnest gesture. "It's like this, Marjorie. As an unknown donor I'll be covered with glory. As a known one I'll be buried under opprobrium."

"'Alas for him who never sees the stars shine through his cypress trees,'" Marjorie quoted lightly with an effort toward bringing Leslie out of her somber mood. "I still advise you to go ahead and not hide your light under a bushel."

"No, I can't," Leslie replied with a trace of her old-time gruffness. "I'm going to tell you a secret. I went to Prexy Matthews last spring and asked him if he would give me a chance to come back to Hamilton and do over my senior year. When I went there I intended to tell him how much it would mean to me on my father's account and of how hard I would try to redeem my past flivvers. He was frosty as a January morning with the mercury way below zero. I had hardly mentioned what I came for when he set his jaws and said that under the circumstances of my expulsion from college he could not for a moment entertain such a request."

"Leslie Cairns!" Marjorie could not repress a sympathetic exclamation.

"It's a fact." The blood rose to Leslie's dark cheeks in a crimson wave. She went on with shamed reluctance. "I thought he might say 'no,' but he made me feel as though he hated even to speak to me. I know I deserved it. I wasn't in his office five minutes hardly. My nerve went back on me. I had to hurry away, or else cry. I didn't have time to tell him anything but that I'd like to try my senior year over again."

"Oh, that was too bad!" Marjorie reached over and laid a consoling hand on one of Leslie's. "Did you go to Hamilton Hall to see him, or to his house?"

"To Hamilton Hall," Leslie returned briefly.

"I am sorry you didn't go to his house instead. It might have made a difference. I can't be sure that it would have," she added honestly.

She was remembering President Matthews' anger at the time of Leslie's expulsion from Hamilton; not only because of the hazing affair in which she and Leslie had figured. There was also the recollection of the misunderstanding which Leslie had made between the president and his old friend, Miss Remson, the manager of Wayland Hall. Again there was the ugly fact of secret collusion between Leslie and Miss Sayres, the president's secretary to be considered.

"Oh, it was too much to expect. I knew Prexy would frown me down without a hearing. But I'd promised myself, that, for my father's sake, there'd be nothing I'd leave undone to make up for the disappointment I caused him," Leslie said with regretful vehemence.

"You were very brave to do it, Leslie." Marjorie's hand tightened its clasp on Leslie's.

"I was glad to try to make amends." Leslie was silent for a moment. "You've never done anything to harm another person, Marjorie," she burst forth. "You can't possibly understand how my heart went down when my father said to me last spring that he had hoped some day to live at Carden Hedge, but that—he'd changed his mind. He never said once: 'It's all your fault.' I wish he had. And I am the one who cheated him of happiness. He'd love to live at the Hedge—if I hadn't made such a mess of things at Hamilton. That's what I did to my father, the person I love best in the world. And all the time I thought I was doing smart things, and getting even with you."

Leslie looked drearily away across the green fleeing landscape, her face bleak and somber.

"Don't feel so crushed, Leslie. You are anxious to please your father. After a while you will find a way. To be willing is half the battle. First thing you know some good will come of it."

"I wish I could make myself believe it." Leslie still kept her head turned away. "The one thing I'd like most to do, I can't do. That's to try over again my senior year at Hamilton. If only Prexy had softened and said I might! After I had been graduated from Hamilton, the way would have been smooth for my father and me to live at the Hedge and be happy. After Prexy turned me down so frigidly I knew he'd never permit my name to be announced at chapel as the giver of the theatre. I'll never put foot on the campus again, not even to see Doris Monroe. Would you?"

"No; not in the present circumstances," Marjorie made frank reply. "There is no reason why you shouldn't come to the Arms to see Miss Susanna and Jerry and me. We'll welcome you."

"I'll come." Leslie brightened. "Mrs. Gaylord and I will have our old apartment at the Hamilton House. There's really no place else for us in Hamilton. I want to stay on there to watch the building of the theatre. My father will be off and away. There is nothing to keep him in a small place like Hamilton. If we lived at the Hedge, he'd be keen on gardening, and beautifying the estate. He'd enjoy the Hamilton links, and probably get up a polo team. He's a wonder at polo."

Leslie clasped her hands behind her head in a quick, nervous motion. She closed her eyes, forcing back the tears which were gathering behind her tightly-shut eyelids.

Marjorie stole a sympathetic, furtive glance at her. She thought the touches of vivid cherry color on Leslie's sleeveless gray wash satin frock charmingly lightened her companion's dark skin and irregular features. She guessed Leslie to be perilously near tears and noted that her subdued pensive expression had softened her face to a peculiar attractiveness.

While Leslie had given up all hope of a return to Hamilton campus as a student, Marjorie was just beginning to consider how such a miracle might be brought to pass. She wondered if an appeal on her part to President Matthews would help Leslie's case. At least she could put forward to the president a generous side of Leslie of which he was not yet aware. She resolved to tell him of Leslie's love for her father, of her deep regret at being unable to make the restitution she so greatly desired to make, of her anxiety to promote his happiness.

Recollection of Doctor Matthews' stern face, on the fateful day when the San Soucians had been arraigned before him and the College Board, returned vividly to Marjorie. For an instant her impulsive determination to seek such an interview with him in behalf of Leslie wavered.

What argument could she present to the learned man of affairs which should be strong enough to justify her request for another trial for Leslie at Hamilton College? She could not but believe that no such request had ever been made to him before. Then, again, Leslie was rated by the Hamilton executive board as the most lawless student who had ever enrolled at that college.

Leslie watched the fleeting scenery as the train rushed eastward, her eyes misted and unseeing. She was not even aware of the shifting panorama of woods, meadows, streams and houses as the train steamed on its way. Instead she was seeing herself as she had been when she flaunted through college, unscrupulous, bullying and untruthful.

She was amazed to think that she had lasted until her senior year. Her one redeeming trait had been her ability to keep up in her classes. She had always been able to make fair recitations on a small amount of study. She wished with desperate fervor now that she had been a "dig" instead of a thorn to the faculty. No; she had been foolish in imagining that she could live down her past unenviable reputation were she to return to the campus.

"Oh!" Marjorie straightened in her chair with a suddenness that made Leslie open her eyes.

"Is that all?" Leslie smiled faintly as she saw Marjorie carefully brush a large cinder from the skirt of her white frock. She folded her hands again behind her head and resumed her dark musing.

Marjorie smiled, too, but said nothing. She might have told Leslie that it was not the appearance of the cinder which had brought forth the "Oh!" She had inadvertently stumbled upon a truth relative to a possible return to the campus of Leslie which she believed could not fail to impress President Matthews.

CHAPTER VI.

LOVE'S YOUNG DREAM

"We are lucky. This is the very kind of night we most wish for our stroll and sail." Marjorie was rejoicing in the beauty of the night as she and Hal walked slowly along over the white sands.

"How could the night be anything but perfect with you home again, Marjorie?" Hal Macy glanced down at the white-clad girl walking beside him as though he contemplated stopping and gathering her in his arms.

"It might be raining torrents, and still I'd have just come home," Marjorie answered in the matter-of-fact tone which had once been Hal's despair. She cast a swift roguish upward glance at her adoring fiancé from under her long curling lashes.

"But it isn't. It couldn't be," Hal tenderly asserted "Say it again, dear. That you are glad to see me; to be walking this old beach again with me. That——"

"I do love to walk this old beach with you—but not too far behind the others. That's the way Connie and Laurie used to do, and then we used to laugh at them," Marjorie gaily assured. "Come on, let's hurry." She ran playfully ahead of Hal, a radiantly pretty figure in the white moonlight.

Hal overtook her in a few long, purposeful strides, saying: "You can't escape me, beautiful moonbeam girl. You are all in white just as you were on that other night last year when you wouldn't let me tell you that I loved you. You've the same kind of soft white scarf over your shoulders, and two stars for eyes. It's you instead of the moonlight who lures my poor heartstrings out of me."

"You have never forgotten that moonlight verse, have you?" Marjorie said lightly. She refused to say that she was pleased to know he had not forgotten it.

"How could I forget it? You quoted it to me on the unhappiest night of my life. Afterward I quoted it you on the happiest night. Is it a wonder—"

"You'd better hurry up if you expect to go sailing this evening," admonished a cheerful, interrupting voice. Unnoticed by the lovers Danny Seabrooke had come up behind them, bent on teasing the absorbed couple.

"You'd better run ahead, Dan-yell, and untie the boat," Hal advised in an anything but sentimental tone.

"You are miles behind the times. Our gallant ship floats free. Only Armitage is getting peeved because he has to hang on to the straining galleon's rope," Danny added with grinning significance.

"Run along and tell him that patience is a virtue," retorted Hal with pleasant irony.

"Tell him yourself when you see him. That will be some time during the evening—we hope. I've run till I'm out of breath. I'm going to poke along with you two. It will be restful—and interesting."

"You may find cause to change your mind," Hal warned darkly.

"Never. Marjorie will protect me." Danny beamed trusting faith at Marjorie. He prudently ranged himself upon her other side, peering timidly forward at Hal, his freckled features alive with ludicrous anxiety.

In the midst of a merry argument between him and Hal the trio arrived at the little pier to which the Oriole, Hal's motor launch, was tied. On the dock three smiling-faced young people awaited Hal and Marjorie. The happiness which Jerry Macy, Constance and Lawrence Armitage felt over the beautiful culmination of Marjorie's and Hal's comradeship was as deep and abiding in its own way as was the love between the newly betrothed pair.

"Such a lovely evening." Jerry greeted them with effusive politeness. "So glad you managed to get here after all."

"You may give *me* credit for rushing 'em to the pier," put in Danny modestly.

"There's plenty of room for an argument, but who wants to argue on a night like this?" Hal returned equably, fixing laughing blue eyes upon Danny.

"You are right, Mr. Macy." Danny made Hal a derisively respectful bow. "I hope others here besides us cherish the same opinion. *You* do, I am sure. *Don't* you, Geraldine?" He turned hopefully to Jerry.

"I don't cherish anything," Jerry returned crushingly.

"Ha-a-a! How sad!" Danny heaved a loud sigh. "What a dreary life you must lead!"

"It suits me," Jerry asserted, with a cheerful smile. "Who's going to take the wheel on the run seaward?" she inquired generally. "Don't all speak at once. Don't speak at all, if you're not crazy for the pilot job. I'd like it, if no one else wants it."

"Oh, if you insist." Laurie Armitage willingly accorded Jerry the wheel. He stood steadying the boat at the little pier while Hal helped the three girls over the side and into the launch.

Constance and Laurie Armitage had lately returned from another year's study of music in Europe. They had not reached Sanford in time to see Marjorie before she had gone West with her father and mother to visit Ronny. In consequence they had looked forward to her sunny presence at Severn Beach with an affectionate impatience second only to Hal's.

"So glad you brought the guitar, Laurie," Marjorie said as Laurie picked it up from the pier floor, where he had laid it briefly, and passed it over the side of the launch to Constance. "Do you know any Spanish songs? I heard such beautiful ones at Manaña."

"Only two or three. We are going to Spain next winter to study the Spanish music and find a very old Spanish opera for Connie, if we can. We found an old music folio in Paris in a queer little odds and ends shop that had three numbers in it from an old Spanish opera called '*la Encantadora*'; the enchantress. Next time we go abroad it will be on the trail of *la Encantadora*," Laurie declared lightly as he stepped into the launch behind the trio of girls.

"Sometime you and Connie must go to Mexico and hunt up some Spanish Mexican music," Marjorie said with enthusiasm. She went on to tell them of how she and Ronny had been serenaded by Teresa's sons and of the tender beauty of the old Spanish song "*Las Estrellas*."

Presently the Oriole was darting seaward in the white moonlight with Jerry at the wheel and Danny beside her entertaining her with his ever ready flow of nonsense. Laurie was lightly strumming the guitar as he waited for Constance to decide upon a song. Marjorie and Hal sat side by side on a long cushioned bench looking like two contented children.

Hal would have been far better content, however, to hold one of Marjorie's hands in his own. He allowed them to lie loosely in her lap because he knew she preferred them to be thus. His Violet Girl did not wear her heart on her sleeve. She treated him with her old-time friendly gaiety, showing only occasional flashes of deeper feeling for him. Hal was confident that Marjorie loved him. Unless she had been very sure of her own heart she would never have given him her promise. Yet the reserve which he had for so long schooled himself to maintain when with her still clung to him.

Constance began the impromptu concert with an old French harvest song which was one of the vocal gems the Armitages had brought to light during the past winter. Laurie accompanied her softly on the guitar, the rhythmic beat of the music blending with the faint wash of the water against the boat's sides. From that she drifted to "Hark, the gentle lark!" and from it to one and another of Brahms' songs, already favorites of the little company.

"The next number of our program will be a touching sentimental song by Dan-yell Seabrooke," Laurie banteringly announced. After singing their old

Brahms' favorite, "The Sapphio Ode," Constance had laughingly gone on a strike, declaring that it was time for someone else to sing.

"What reason have you to suspect that it will be?" Danny fixed a severe gaze upon Laurie. "Do I *look* sentimental? Do I *act* sentimental? Do I *seem* sentimental?"

"Nothing like trying." Laurie ignored the forceful interrogations. "If you try, and don't succeed—" He made a motion as of pitching something over the boat's side into the water.

"Nev-vur! I shall succeed; if not in singing, then in dodging," Danny averred with great resolution. "Hand me the guitar. I wouldn't trust you with it in such an emergency. You might play off the key and spoil my song."

"Is that so? What about my risk in handing you the guitar and having it spoiled?"

"About fifty-fifty, I should say." Danny grinned amiably and reached for the guitar. He pretended to tune it, grumbling. Presently in the midst of his pretense of disfavor he surprised his smiling companions with the charming prelude of "What does your heart say?" a popular baritone solo from "The Orchid," a New York musical success.

It was the first time that any of the five listeners to Danny had ever heard him seriously attempt a sentimental song. Possessed of a tuneful baritone voice Danny had earned a reputation among his friends as a singer of comic songs. Hal and Laurie regarded the departure merely as a decidedly successful attempt upon Danny's part to make good. Into Marjorie's and Constance's minds, however, the thought sprang instantly that Danny was deeply in love—with Jerry, of course.

As for Jerry! She was hoping no one could see the added color in her cheeks by the bright moonlight. During Danny's rendition of the song she had occupied herself industriously with the wheel, her round, babyish face as nearly a blank as she could make it. Danny hardly ended the solo when she began clapping her hands in light applause.

"Bravo! You win!" she called out. "You certainly gave a fine imitation of a sentimental warbler, Dan-yell. Laurie didn't think you could do it."

"Oh, I have nerve enough for anything," Danny retorted. "What does Mr. Lawrence Armitage know of my talents and capabilities?"

"Not a thing, thank fortune," asserted Laurie with stress.

"You may have your guitar. I wouldn't sing you another song if you begged me to. I am going to devote myself to Geraldine. She never treats me kindly, but she's an improvement upon you." Danny wisely produced this plea as an excuse to seat himself close to the wheel and Jerry.

She received him without comment, pretending to be listening to the buzz of conversation going on among the others. Laurie was running a series of chords up and down the guitar strings which had an oddly familiar sound both to her ears and Marjorie's. He continued sounding them a moment or two, then glanced at Hal, nodding.

Suddenly Hal's sweet echoing tenor voice lifted itself on the moonlit air in a lilting melody that Marjorie had good cause to remember.

"Down the center, little one,

Life for us has just begun!"

Hal was singing the quaint words of the Irish Minuet. To Marjorie it would ever be the song of songs. Like the prince's kiss which had wakened the sleeping beauty from her enchanted sleep, sound of it had awakened her dreaming heart and opened her ears to the voice of love.

Involuntarily she stretched forth a hand until it rested lightly upon one of the singer's. Instantly Hal had caught it, holding it in his own. He bent an adoring glance upon her, and sang on.

"This was what I was wishing for," he declared fondly the moment he had finished the song. He gathered her slim hand more closely in his own. "I hardly dared take it with everybody looking on, for fear you'd not wish it."

"It was dear in you to sing that, Hal." The eyes of the pair met in a long fond glance of affection. "You know I shall always love it best of all songs. You understand why."

"Yes, dear." There was quiet rapture in the response. "I forgot to send back the music to it to Leila last spring. So I brought it to the Beach for Laurie to play. I thought you'd like to hear it again."

"I love it. Think how much of happiness we owe Leila Greatheart. If it had not been for her Irish play you would never have come to Hamilton. You'd probably have gone to Alaska, as you had planned to do."

"I had begun to feel that I couldn't bear to see you for a while, knowing you didn't love me," Hal confessed. "I knew I'd never stop caring for you. I was sure it was the only thing for me to do."

"I'm so glad you didn't go. You see, Hal, I should have known later—that I cared—perhaps too late." Marjorie's lovely features shadowed. "I had begun to know that I missed you, and I'd read Brooke Hamilton's journal and had felt a kind of terrible despair over it. He hadn't understood Angela's love for him until after her serious illness. Just when he was beginning to be happy he lost her. I couldn't help wondering if it would be so with me. Brooke Hamilton helped us to our happiness. On that account there is something I'd like to do—I know it would please Miss Susanna. It's about—about our wedding."

"Our wedding." Hal repeated the two magic words in a kind of beatified daze. "What about our wedding, dearest. Are you going to tell me that you've changed your mind and are going to marry me in the fall instead of next June?" There was a suppressed, hopeful note in the question.

"Not in the fall, or next June, either." Marjorie's up-flashing smile did not match her negative answer. "I can't desert Hamilton until the dormitory is finished and dedicated and the biography completed. And there's the Leila Harper Playhouse, too. So it couldn't possibly be in the fall. But"—Marjorie made a tiny pause—"I think my work at Hamilton will have been completed by the last of next April." She made another brief pause, then said with direct simplicity: "I'd like our wedding to take place on the evening of May Day, at Hamilton Arms. May Day was Brooke Hamilton's birthday."

"Marjorie!" Hal exclaimed very softly. He caught Marjorie's free hand, then prisoned both her hands between his own. "My heart went down when you said 'not next June.' But the first of May! That is sooner than I had hoped for. You can depend upon Miss Susanna to back that plan. She'll be delighted. How about General and Captain? Have you told them yet?"

"No." Marjorie shook her curly head. "Not yet. There is to be a grand Dean confab tomorrow morning right after breakfast. Oh, I know they will be willing to give up having the wedding at Castle Dean. In some ways I'd love to be married from my dear pretty home in Sanford where our old crowd had such good times. But the Arms has an even stronger claim upon me. I want to make Miss Susanna happy. She has been so wonderful to Hamilton College, and to me," Marjorie ended eloquently.

Hal's approval of her idea was not expressed in words. It came in the tightening of his hands on Marjorie's and the glance of unutterable devotion which he bent upon her.

"You see, Hal," Marjorie said after a short interval of rapt silence between them, "Hamilton Arms has become like a second home to me. I'm not afraid Miss Susanna would object to the fuss and decorating that must naturally go with a house wedding. She'd love it, because she loves us. I thought it all out when I was at Manaña. That is, the main points. Violets were Brooke Hamilton's favorite flowers, and you call me your Violet girl. So I am going to have a violet wedding in the spring when there are loads of double, sweet-scented violets in bloom at the Arms."

Completely absorbed in each other, Hal and Marjorie had drifted far away from the amused quartette of friends who were considerately ignoring their presence. While their friends kept up a lively murmur of conversation the lovers floated far and free upon the boundless sea of romance with love for their pilot.

"If they should come back this evening I'll see that Macy takes his trick at the wheel," Danny said to Jerry in a purposeful undertone.

"Oh, they won't be back until someone leads them off the Oriole onto the pier." Jerry's reply was full of deep satisfaction. Marjorie's final awakening to love for Hal would ever be a blessed marvel to Jerry. "What's the matter with my steering? Don't you like it?" she demanded of Danny.

"I have a high opinion of it," Danny hastily assured. "Only I hate to see you so overworked. I should enjoy having you sit beside me on that bench over there, and holding your hand. I should enjoy——"

"I shouldn't enjoy having you," Jerry interrupted cruelly.

"Say not so. You have never trusted me with your nice plump little hand. I would be very careful of it," he added ingratiatingly.

"No thank you. I'd rather be excused."

"Why would you?" Danny persisted with an interested inquiring grin.

Jerry had to laugh. "How can I tell?" she countered. She felt the color rise to her cheeks, and was glad Danny couldn't detect it by moonlight.

"You can't—not until you've tried holding hands with me," Danny asserted with a wise air.

"Some other time," Jerry made indefinite, careless promise.

"No time like the present." One of Danny's hands suddenly covered one of Jerry's as it rested on the wheel. "You wouldn't be so mean as to leave me out of this hand-holding party, would you?" he asked, an undercurrent of seriousness in his bantering tones.

"No," replied Jerry with sudden shy brevity. And for the remainder of the ride the Oriole had the advantage of double handpower at the wheel.

CHAPTER VII.

A BIT OF NEWS

"And Fifteen is vacant, you say? How queer." Marjorie commented, her eyes on Leila Harper, who was arranging a row of glasses on her study table preparatory to filling them with imported ginger ale.

"As queer as the pea green hat that Mother Molly O'Toole found hanging on a gooseberry bush the day before the fair at Dongerry," agreed Leila Harper with her broadest smile. She kept on smiling as she recited in her inimitable Celtic accent:

"Acushla, 'twas near to the day of the fair

And poor Mother Molly'd no bonnet to wear,

Except a frilled cap she had worn day by day,

And year after year in the same humble way.

She went out of doors, and she heaved such a sigh

She blew up a gale in the garden near-by,

It whisked a wee leprechaun out of a tree

He lost his green hat as away he did flee:

It hung on the bush where the gooseberries grew;

Next morn Molly found it all covered with dew.

She dried it, 'twas grandly becoming to wear,

And she took a fine prize at the Dongerry fair."

"Certainly some remarkable things have happened in Ireland," Muriel Harding declared mischievously. "Please, Irish witch woman, may I pass the glasses?"

"You may; but spill not a drop out of one of them," Leila cautioned. She picked up a cake knife from the table and flourished it over a huge black chocolate cake with thick white icing.

"You haven't told me yet how it happens that Fifteen is vacant, Leila Greatheart," Marjorie reminded.

"In a minute. Let me start Midget going with the cake and I will tell you anything," was Leila's rash promise.

"Whether you know it or not," slyly added Ronny Lynne.

"Whether I know it or not," Leila repeated firmly.

A burst of laughter rose from her six companions. The little group of seven girls who had been the first Travelers at Hamilton College five years before were gathered once more in the room occupied by Leila Harper and Vera Mason at Wayland Hall during that long happy period. It lacked only a few days of the formal opening of Hamilton College and the seven post-graduates were already back on the campus eager to begin what would undoubtedly be to them their most momentous year at Hamilton College.

Readers of the "MARJORIE DEAN HIGH SCHOOL SERIES," "THE MARJORIE DEAN COLLEGE SERIES" and "THE MARJORIE DEAN POST GRADUATE SERIES," each comprising four volumes, have followed Marjorie through many of her girlhood adventures as a student, first at Sanford High School, later at Hamilton College, where she found her work and brought happiness to Miss Susanna Hamilton, the embittered great-niece of Brooke Hamilton, who was the distinguished founder of Hamilton College.

Marjorie, having been chosen by Miss Susanna as best fitted, in her estimation, to write the biography of Brooke Hamilton, had returned to Hamilton Arms once more there to bring to completion the delightful literary task she had begun the previous March.

As yet, her General and her Captain alone were in possession of her plan for a violet wedding at the Arms on the evening of May Day. Miss Susanna had not yet been made acquainted with what would seem to her a visitation of good fortune. Marjorie was saving the request she purposed to make of her devoted friend until a particularly propitious occasion.

"Hurry and pass the cake, Vera. This tyrannical Celtic person says you must before she will tell us a thing," Marjorie urged, laughing.

"Here, help yourselves." Vera hastily set the plate of cake Leila had handed her upon the table with a hospitable gesture. "You can't even have paper plates to put it on. We forgot to buy them. We used to boast of four china plates, but our guests are so rough."

"Too bad. Never mind. Luciferous has a notebook. Delighted, Luciferous." Muriel laid calm hold upon the notebook in Lucy's hand. "Yes, you must," she said with reproving stress as Lucy clung to the book. She captured it, tore sheets of paper from it and handed them round to the tune of Lucy's grumbling at such a waste of good paper. "Just as good as plates," Muriel declared jovially. She hastily transferred a slice of cake to her make-shift plate and beamed encouragingly upon Leila.

Leila returned the smile in kind. "The reason Fifteen is still vacant," she began, "is because no one has applied for it. Now what could be queerer?"

"*Not anyone?*" Jerry Macy's eyes grew round.

"Not anyone. All Miss Remson's other vacancies have been filled. She thinks it is odd, but she doesn't mind. She will probably have an application for it soon. It is a very desirable room, you know."

"We surely do," Marjorie and Jerry answered in merry chorus.

"Perhaps two girls from one of the other campus houses may hear it is vacant and take it. Undoubtedly they will. It will never go begging," was Jerry's opinion.

"Fifteen is one of the best rooms at the Hall. We can speak from experience, can't we, estimable Bean?" Jerry remarked, turning humorous eyes upon Marjorie.

"*Can we?*" Marjorie returned the glance of affection. "When will Miss Remson be home, Leila? It seems odd to come back to the Hall and not see her first thing."

The five Sanford chums had arrived at Hamilton late on the previous afternoon. They had been met at the Hamilton station by Leila and Vera and triumphantly whisked to Hamilton Arms in Vera's car. There Miss Susanna Hamilton had been awaiting their arrival with fond impatience. Exuberant celebration had followed their arrival at the Arms. There had been a delightful dinner in the famous Chinese room and the buoyant guests had remained at the Arms overnight.

It was now early afternoon of the next day. Marjorie and Jerry had come over to Wayland Hall for one of their old-time social sessions in Leila's and Vera's rooms. The latter had returned from a summer spent in Ireland over a week previous to the Sanford girls' arrival on the campus. They had come direct from the big ocean steamer to Hamilton campus and Wayland Hall.

"She'll be here tomorrow." Miss Remson, the brisk little manager of the Hall, was away on a brief vacation of a week at the seashore. "She was going to refuse an old friend's invitation on account of expecting you girls. Midget and I made her change her mind, and go."

"I'm so glad that you did," Marjorie returned. "I'm anxious to see her. I hope two dandy girls will take Fifteen."

"We shall need them," Leila said with a suspicion of dryness.

"Why do you say that, Leila Greatheart?" A little pucker of anxiety showed itself upon Marjorie's smooth forehead. "You must have some very good reason for such an opinion."

"I have," Leila made prompt reply. "There is still danger at the Hall of the calamity of the house divided against itself."

"Isn't there less now than when Muriel was on the outs with the Ice Queen and the Ice Queen was on the outs with Gentleman Gus and the Bertramites?" Ronny humorously referred to the Travelers' vernacular in the way of names. "This year, remember, they will all stand shoulder to shoulder with us."

"You forget the Screech Owl, who was born a gossip and a disturber," Leila reminded with a frown. "She was on her good behavior last spring when she had a part in my Irish play. Did not I write the part of the village gossip for her, on purpose, that she might see herself? She saw nothing but her own glory as an actress. But she was so pleased that she talked of herself and not of anyone else for a while. This much good I did. But I happen to know she went back to gossiping again."

"Whom did she gossip about? Doris? She naturally would, since Doris had cut her acquaintance," Muriel showed considerable interest. "That was directly after the Rustic Romp, you know. They disagreed over Leslie Cairns."

"That was precisely where the shoe pinched," Leila asserted. "It was Leslie Cairns who Miss Peyton chose to blame for her falling out with Doris. Then she could not resist the temptation to be spiteful."

"What did Miss Peyton say about Leslie?" Marjorie asked with a suspicion of troubled annoyance in her question.

"What you might expect. That she had attended the Rustic Romp. That fine bit of news came to me through Miss Crawford, on the day before college closed," Leila said sarcastically. "She came to me and asked me in horrified tones if it were true that Miss Dean had smuggled Miss Cairns, an expelled student, into the gym on the night of the Romp."

"Who could have told Miss Crawford that except Miss Peyton?" Vera cried indignantly. "And why should she start such a tale about Marjorie?"

"Because she is still angry with me," Marjorie returned composedly. "She wanted Jane to blow the whistle for unmasking. I asked Jane to wait a little. Miss Peyton does not know positively that Leslie was at the Romp."

"That's exactly the point. She has no real ground for circulating that story. It's unjust to Marjorie. There has been too much of such unfairness in the past." Leila's lips set in a forbidding line.

"Don't worry about it for a minute, Leila Greatheart," said Marjorie soothingly. "I mean about anything Miss Peyton may choose to say of me. We'll have to try to conquer her by winning over the Hall to our code of ethics. When she discovers that no one likes to hear gossip, perhaps she will stop gossiping."

"That's a fine, rosy Bean view of things. But will it ever come true?" Jerry propounded, tilting her head to one side and rolling doubtful eyes.

"It won't if you scoff at it, and treat it lightly," Marjorie retorted.

"Depend on the Screech Owl to start something. Screech Owl!" Muriel repeated the name with mock admiration. "What could be more appropriate? My nobility doesn't extend to refraining from that fond title."

"*You* are gossiping." Lucy Warner pointed an accusing finger at Muriel.

"*Never.* Truth is truth, no matter where 'tis uttered. I'm merely saying to you girls what I should take great pleasure in saying to the Screech Owl herself. I long to tell her her right name." Muriel accompanied her fervent declaration with a sweeping gesture.

"Perhaps vacation joys will make her forget the Rustic Romp and what she thinks she knows about Leslie," Ronny made light prediction.

"Very optimistic, but not at all likely," was Vera's opinion.

"How did you answer Miss Crawford, Leila." Marjorie had missed most of the gay exchange of raillery among her companions. Her brain was busy with the same problem that had invaded her thoughts on the last afternoon she and Leslie Cairns had been together on the Speedwell.

"I asked her a question in return for hers. I said: 'Who told you that such a thing had happened?' She tossed her head and said: 'I prefer not to answer that question.' Then I smiled at her with fine Celtic good humor, and said: 'And I prefer not to answer yours.' It was on the campus near the Bean holder that we met. She walked away in a miff. And I have not seen her since," Leila ended genially.

"It's too bad." Marjorie stared at Leila with a troubled air.

"Now why should it be?" Leila demanded, smiling. "I have no admiration for Miss Crawford, nor never did have. She is too ready to believe unpleasant gossip."

"I'm not thinking of Miss Crawford. I'm thinking of Leslie." Marjorie's winsome smile broke out.

"I suspected that you had sympathy for someone besides me. I kept quiet out of Irish politeness." Despite her light retort Leila was surveying Marjorie with true Celtic shrewdness. She knew Marjorie to be at the point of announcing something of especial import.

The other girls were hardly less keen at reading the signs and arriving at the same conclusion. Thus far none of her chums knew of the intimate conversation she and Leslie Cairns had held on that last memorable afternoon the two girls had spent on the observation platform of Peter Cairns' private car. Marjorie had regarded it in the light of a secret confidence. Now, however, she had decided to impart it to the little group of Travelers as a matter of interest to Leslie. The six Travelers present already knew of the part Leslie Cairns had played the previous spring in the Rustic Romp. Leslie had requested Marjorie to tell her intimates of the affair. "I'd like your Beanstalks to know the rights of that performance," she had said to Marjorie with a tinge of humor.

"Girls;" Marjorie's clear decided intonation brought all eyes to bear upon her; "Leslie Cairns wants just one thing above all others that I wish we could help her to gain. She wants to come back to the campus and do her senior year over again."

CHAPTER VIII.

PLEDGED TO STAND BY

"What?" Jerry allowed the cake knife in her hand to drop squarely upon the cake. She had been poising it over the big square delicacy preparatory to replenishing the cake plate. In her surprise she vented Leslie Cairns' own pet ejaculation.

"Good night!" Muriel Harding pretended collapse in her chair.

"I am afraid she is courting the impossible." Vera Mason shook her head.

"There's something in your tone, Beauty, that makes me think it might not be impossible." Leila was regarding Marjorie with a quizzical smile. "Yet for the life of me I cannot see how it might happen."

"I'm not in the least sure that it could," was Marjorie's candid reply. "I had thought that as soon as Prexy came back to the campus I would go to him and put in a plea for Leslie. I have in mind certain arguments that might appeal to him. In thinking about her I have realized, that, if he gave her permission to enroll again she would have to go through a good deal of unpleasantness on the campus. I realized it more when Leila was telling us about what Miss Crawford had said."

"It might not be so terribly hard for her, Marjorie. She wouldn't try, of course, to live on the campus. Her father would undoubtedly open Carden Hedge." Ronny took this cheerful view of the matter.

"No; Leslie says if she could try her senior year over she would not risk living at the Hedge for fear a lot of things about her old lawless days on the campus might come up and be talked over. Then her father would probably be criticized for her bad behavior. She says she couldn't bear that."

"She could live at the Hamilton House and get away with it," Muriel said confidently. "She could arrange her program so as to go from one class to another without having to stay on the campus a moment longer than recitation hours."

"She made satisfactory recitations in the old days," Leila remarked musingly. "I used to wonder how she did it. She was always out in her car or entertaining at Baretti's, or the Colonial."

"She was within two months of being graduated from Hamilton when the sword fell," Vera reminded.

"The trouble is," Marjorie drew a regretful breath, "she has already been to Prexy about it."

"She has?" rose a concerted cry.

Marjorie nodded soberly. "He wouldn't listen to her," she continued. "She was so hurt and confused at his brusqueness that she didn't try to explain at all why she wanted to come back to the campus. That was the very thing that might have influenced President Matthews to give her another trial."

"This *is* news," Leila emphasized. "How can one help but admire Leslie Cairns for her courage in facing Prexy. I believe now she may turn out well."

Marjorie smiled. She wondered what Leila would say could she have even an inkling of the wonderful plan Leslie had in view for her. "She is brave as can be," she agreed. "I feel as though she hadn't had a fair opportunity to soften the hard heart of Prexy. That is the reason I am going to brave Prexy in his den all by myself. Miss Susanna offered to go with me. Then we talked it over and decided I had best go alone. What do you think, Lucy? Is there any possibility that Prexy might change his mind about Leslie? You know him better than we."

"Yes, Luciferous Warniferous, high and exalted scribe of the Prexy realm, speak, and tell us the worst," Muriel made a commanding gesture at which Lucy merely giggled.

"I don't know what to say." Her small face suddenly sobered. "Prexy is the kindest man I know until he has been really shocked by something that someone has done. Then he grows terribly stern. He was angrier about the trouble Leslie Cairns made between him and Miss Remson than the hazing. Yet he will do more for you, Marjorie, than he would for almost anyone else. You may be able to persuade him to give Leslie another trial. But—" She came to an abrupt pause, her green eyes fastened peculiarly upon Marjorie's face with eloquent significance.

"I understand you, Lucy. You are right. I shouldn't care to have Prexy offer Leslie another trial just to please me. The only way for him to offer it to her is because he has become convinced that it is the best thing to do."

"And that will be your job, Bean—to convince Prexy that second thoughts are best. Such an easy little task," Jerry declared satirically. "You certainly have had some splendid jobs since you came to Hamilton. I feel the inspiration stealing over me to jingle. Ahem! Aha! Bzzz-zz! Whir-r-r! Br-rr-p!"

"No easy task, it is to ask,

Our Prexy to relent,

Smile on, serene, undaunted Bean,

Until he has unbent."

"That is good advice, Jeremiah. I shall proceed to follow it," laughed Marjorie.

"And I shall proceed to copy the jingle." Leila confiscated another sheet of paper from Lucy's notebook and jotted down the jingle. She smiled widely to herself as she wrote. Leila had a plan of her own regarding Jerry's jingles which she intended to carry out presently.

"I shall go to see President Matthews as soon as he returns from the shore. That will be the last of the week. I'll wait until Monday to make my call," Marjorie announced decisively.

"If I were you I should go to his house, Marjorie," Lucy advised in her serious fashion. "It's more quiet at his home office. At Hamilton Hall he has so many interruptions. Persons are continually passing in and out of his office."

"That was what I thought. And if I should succeed—" Marjorie broke off. Her brown eyes traveled from one face to another in the group. "I was thinking of what Muriel said about Leslie hurrying away from the campus as soon as her classes were over. As good Travelers we couldn't let her do that. If she comes back to the senior class we must stand by her on all occasions. I know a way in which we could help her a great deal. We could ask her to belong to the Travelers."

"Whu-u-u!" Muriel emitted a prolonged sigh of surprise. A united murmur went up from the others.

"Is that a murmur of objection?" Marjorie asked with a little laugh.

"No," was the ascending hearty protest.

"You simply stunned us for a second, Beauty," Leila said reassuringly. "Stop and think if it is not an amazing idea that Leslie Cairns should become a member of the Travelers. Consider all the past troubles she has caused that worthy organization." She showed her white teeth in an amused smile.

"Do you mean *our* Nineteen?" Muriel could not keep a faint note of amazement, bordering on disapproval out of her question.

"She couldn't very well belong to either of the other chapters," Jerry pointed out. "The only members of last year's Travelers at Hamilton to be here this year will be Phil Moore and Barbara Severn. Oh, yes. Anna Towne is coming back to teach English Literature. The new Travelers were all chosen before college closed last June, weren't they?" She turned inquiringly to Marjorie.

"Yes. The only Travelers' chapter Leslie could very well belong to would be ours. Of course all this is only tentative. If Prexy declines to do anything for Leslie it would be of no use to ask her to join the Travelers."

"The Board would have to give consent as well as Prexy to her coming back," Vera interposed.

"Yes, but I dare say the Board members would if President Matthews recommended another trial for her," Marjorie answered.

"Did you ever hear of an ex-Hamilton student being permitted to return to Hamilton again?" Ronny asked dubiously.

"No, I never have. Perhaps this will be the first case of the kind on the Hamilton records," Marjorie replied brightly. "I wish you girls would tell me exactly the way you feel about helping Leslie Cairns if she should come back to college."

"Just the way you do, I hope," Vera made loyal return.

"It is a fine diversion you are providing for my old age," was Leila's mock-enthusiastic response. "But I can stand it, if you can, Beauty."

"Yours truly." Muriel thus pledged her devotion. "Doris would be glad of it. She really cares a good deal for Leslie Cairns."

"You should have more faith in your pals," Ronny rebuked with simulated severity. "When have we ever gone back on you?"

"I wish there was something I could say to President Matthews that would help," was Lucy's regretful cry.

"Is it necessary for me to say, Bean, dear Bean, that I will never desert you?" Jerry contributed reproachfully.

"You are darling old dears." Marjorie beamed warmest affection on the group of white-clad girls who had just sworn fealty afresh to her standard.

"And you are the same beautiful Beauty that you were five years ago when you walked into Baretti's one fine September evening and began the conquest of Leslie Cairns which has ended in her unconditional surrender." Leila was looking a world of affectionate admiration at Marjorie. "Did I not say to you then, Midget, that Beauty had arrived on the campus, and that great doings would come to pass?"

"You surely did say it, and that is at least one of your prophesies which has come true," Vera made ready response.

"Nonsense. It was not I. It was my faithful Beanstalks. What could I have done for democracy without them? You are the same splendid Leila Harper, who worked like mad to make things come right on the campus and then wouldn't believe she'd done anything worth while. You see I can say as much about you as you said about me," Marjorie triumphantly retaliated. "Who was it—."

"Never mind who it was," Leila cut in hastily. "Let us talk of the campus. It is a beautiful piece of ground. Is it not?" She inquired of Marjorie with polite affability. "Have I not heard you say you admire it?"

"I wish I could see it from my windows at Hamilton Arms," Marjorie said half wistfully, though she smiled at Leila's ridiculous air and questions. "I do miss you girls and the Hall and the campus dreadfully, much as I love the Arms. It was fine, you know, to be right in the middle of the campus, as it were. I shan't settle down again at the biography much before the first of November. As soon as Robin comes back, Page and Dean will have to get busy in the show business again."

"Robin ought to be here by this time. We received a letter from her just before we sailed for home in which she wrote that she was coming back to Hamilton as early as the first of September." Vera gave out this news as she hospitably replenished the glasses from the case of ginger ale on the floor.

"She has probably waited for Phil, and Phil may have been delayed by an influx of visiting relatives," was Marjorie's guess. "The Moores are the most hospitable of southerners Robin says."

"It will be a week before the campus begins to be inhabited," Ronny predicted. "Then the campus dwellers will arrive in numbers. Did you and Vera see Doris Monroe while you were abroad, Leila? Of course you had her Paris address."

"We spent three days with her in Paris. She was with an aunt in a cunning little apartment in the Rue de Rivoli. Her father and his party of explorers have unearthed a buried city in Peru. He will not return to France for another year." Vera went on to relate the details of their visit to Doris Monroe. She ended with: "Doris must be on the way across the Atlantic now. She was intending to sail for the United States the first of September."

"What news from the Bertramites?" asked Muriel.

"None," replied Leila. "That means you may expect them to come breezing back to Hamilton any day. Kathie and Lillian will be here on next Friday evening, according to Kathie's letter. And now are you not glad that I would tell you nothing about the campus news last night?" Leila viewed her friends with indulgently twinkling eyes.

On the previous evening she had laughingly refused to give out a word of information concerning campus matters. "If Midget and I were to tell you all the news tonight we should have nothing to entertain you with at the Hall tomorrow," she had argued.

Leila's good-humored inquiry evoked a buzz of laughing rejoinders. "I am so kind," she continued, "I will keep on giving you the news. Besides you girls and ourselves there are only four other students back at the Hall; Miss Peters and Miss Finch, those two nice freshies who had last year, and Miss Keller and Miss Ryan, the two sophs who roomed next to Miss Peyton and Miss Carter. They are sophs and juniors now, but their hats will continue to fit their heads, I believe. Let me see. Midget and I have only half unpacked our trunks. We have done a great deal of visiting at the Arms, and no work."

"Tomorrow we are going to clean house and unpack and buy some plates at the ten cent store. Lead really useful lives, you know," Vera announced with joking energy.

"Midget is that ambitious!" Leila became colloquially Celtic.

Vera's light announcement brought forth plenty of similar jesting resolves from the others. With conversation flowing in a purely personal channel Leslie Cairns' name was not mentioned again. Having pledged their word to do all they could to help her six of the reunited Travelers were only too well content to allow the subject to drop. They had not yet come to the stage of regarding Leslie from Marjorie's great-spirited viewpoint.

Of them all Vera was the nearest to Marjorie in tolerance. She was willing to help Leslie for Leslie's sake; not because of her regard for Marjorie. With the others it was solely on Marjorie's account that they had agreed to stand by Leslie, should future need of their support arise. Jerry and Ronny, the only ones besides Marjorie who knew of Leslie's plan for Leila, had at heart not yet entirely forgiven Leslie for past offenses against Marjorie. Muriel Harding would probably never cherish any degree of liking for Leslie, no matter how well she might do in future. Muriel had a peculiarly obdurate side of character in spite of her natural sunnyness of disposition.

As for Leila, only Leila herself knew how greatly she still detested Leslie Cairns. Though she had been first to credit Leslie for her courage in seeking President Matthews, even this incident had not altered in the slightest degree her basic dislike for the financier's once lawless daughter. Her secret aversion for Leslie had not died with the knowledge of the other girl's change of heart.

Once before Leila had found occasion to admire Leslie's moral courage, tardily as it had shown itself. This was on the day in spring when she and Marjorie had encountered Leslie Cairns on the road to Orchard Inn and the latter had halted their car to make brave confession to Marjorie. In spite of it Leila had not warmed toward the penitent then. Nor had this latest report of Leslie's courage stirred in Leila any real sympathy. Leila would not have admitted such an attitude of mind, even to Vera. For Marjorie's sake she was resolved to hide her dislike for Leslie so securely that no one should even suspect her of it.

CHAPTER IX.

A MOMENTOUS ERRAND

"How do I look, Jeremiah? Very grave and serious, I hope." Marjorie walked sedately to the center of the spacious sitting room which was a part of hers and Jerry's luxurious quarters at Hamilton Arms. She paused, casting an interrogative glance at Jerry, who was sitting on the edge of a chair interestingly following Marjorie's every movement.

"You don't look half as solemn as you think you feel," was Jerry's opinion delivered with a faint chuckle.

"How discouraging." Marjorie stopped before the long plate glass wall mirror for a last critical inspection. She thought she made a really unobtrusive appearance in her plain dark blue faille gown and small blue faille hat.

"You might better wear your new jade afternoon frock with the black fur bands," Jerry grumbled critically. "The world is yours in that rig."

"You're a fond goose, Jeremiah. It has to be a case of 'I won't speak of myself' today. I wish to eliminate Marjorie Dean from the situation as thoroughly as I can. I wish Prexy's interest to be all for Leslie. The color of my new dress might interfere with his thought processes. This is strictly a matter of psychology, you know," she declared gaily.

"All right, Bean. You win. You look almost as beautiful as ever, if not more so. True beauty cannot be hidden." Jerry rose in a declamatory attitude, one arm raised stiffly. "It peereth forth from even the humblest of blue faille—"

"Stop it this instant." Marjorie forgot sedateness and rushed upon Jerry, open-armed. Jerry threw up both arms and accidentally knocked Marjorie's hat off. "Now see what you've done." Laughing, Marjorie straightened a dent in her little blue hat and went over to the mirror to readjust it. "You've completely chased away my seriousness, Jeremiah Macy."

"A good thing. Don't worry about the way you ought to approach Prexy. Whatever you say to him will be the best thing that could possibly be said for Leslie." This time it was Jerry who turned momentarily serious.

"I hope so." Marjorie gave a quick, longing sigh. "Now I must be on my way. Lucy said Prexy would surely be at the house after four today. It's a quarter to four now. I'll meet you at Wayland Hall at five o'clock. Coming down stairs with me?"

"No. I've a letter to write. I must start it this minute. It's to Hal. Any messages," she called slyly. Marjorie was at the door.

"Not any." Marjorie laughed and blushed charmingly. "Good-bye, Jeremiah. See you later." She tripped down the broad staircase and into the library where Miss Susanna Hamilton sat at the long mahogany table busily occupied with sorting the loose yellow leaves of an old book.

"So you are off on the momentous errand, are you, child?" she greeted, her eyes still on her dilettante task. She laid down the leaf in her hand and turned her keen dark eyes smilingly upon Marjorie. "What a plain little dress! But I like it. It's suitable to the errand on which you are going. Marvelous Manager with no frills or furbelows."

"If I succeed with Prexy this afternoon I shall feel that I can lay claim to that ridiculous title for just once." Marjorie came over to Miss Hamilton. She bent and kissed the old lady's pink cheek. "Please don't be lonely without us at dinner tonight, Goldendede," she said. "Remember we'll all be here tomorrow night for a regular Travelers' reunion."

"Run along, my dear. I'll be glad to be rid of both you and Jerry this evening," chuckled Miss Susanna. "Think what an opportunity I shall have to collate this book, uninterrupted."

"Good-bye." Marjorie started for the door in pretended offense. Half way across the library she paused, looking back and laughing.

"Wait a minute, Marjorie. Try not to feel downcast if President Matthews should be brusque with you in regard to Leslie," was the older woman's advice. "He is broader-minded than most presidents of colleges that I have known. And I have known a good many of them. They are all alike in their deep disapproval of particularly lawless students. Leslie's case seems very doubtful to me. I don't mean to be discouraging. I know how strongly prejudiced such men are against flagrant student offenders."

"I understand." Marjorie gave a little comprehending nod. She came back and kissed Miss Susanna again, saying: "Wish me good fortune, Goldendede. I'm going on a quick hike to a trying engagement."

"Good luck attend you, Lieutenant Dean." Miss Susanna watched the trim little figure across the room and through the open door.

Marjorie left the Arms and sped lightly down the wide stone walk to the gates. She was soon swinging along with her free buoyant stride through picturesque Hamilton Estates and toward the campus. For a little the tender beauty of the early September day caused her to forget her errand in fervent Nature worship. Overhead the sun's golden gleams filtered down from skies of palest blue between snatches of drifting, snowy clouds. The sweeping lawns and gardens of the Estates were bright with scarlet sage, dahlias and early autumn flowers. Along the sides of the pike and in the fields grew goldenrod, daisies and purple asters in Nature's own profusion. Here and there the foliage of a tree had been touched by magic fingers and turned from green to red and gold.

Marjorie greeted the emerald-hued campus with a fond smile and a soft: "You're as splendid as ever, old friend." She entered the east gates and followed the drive for a little way, then left it to travel straight across the broad green sweep toward President Matthews' house which was situated at the extreme west side of the campus.

It was now almost a week since the initial band of Travelers had gathered at the Hall and Marjorie had then announced her determination to go to President Matthews in behalf of Leslie Cairns. She had been obliged to delay her call upon the President for the very good reason that he had not returned to Hamilton campus from the sea shore until Tuesday of that week. It was now Thursday. The next day, Friday, would see the return of Katherine Langly and Lillian Wenderblatt to the campus. There was to be a jolly celebration at the Arms on Friday evening in honor of them. In view of happiness so near at hand Marjorie was desirous of immediately putting Leslie's case before the President and having the self-appointed interview with "Prexy" off her mind.

As she crossed the broad green, endeared by long familiarity to her feet, her gaze wandered from one to another of the campus houses. Her eyes brightened to see three girls seated on the steps of Craig Hall. At Acasia House a slim girl shape stood on the top step of the front veranda, waving an arm at an expressman coming up the walk with a heavy-looking trunk. In front of Silverton Hall three girls were emerging from a taxicab. Marjorie stopped to stare at them. No; they were not Phyllis Moore, Barbara Severn and Robin Page. She was not sure of their identity. She experienced a glad sense of happiness at the thought that the campus dwellers were gathering home again. The end of another week and Hamilton Campus would have again become its old delightful center of activity.

As she turned in at the gateway of the ornamental hedge which surrounded the president's home, Marjorie's buoyant interest in the campus receded and was replaced by the graver import of her errand. She hoped she would find the president alone. Perhaps Lucy would be there. Lucy had been working for him for the past two days.

"I shan't mind if Lucy is there," Marjorie was thinking as she neared the steps. Her heart was beating uncomfortably fast. She had a strong inclination to turn and run away. She did not dread the coming interview. What she did dread was the probable event of defeat.

CHAPTER X.

FOR LESLIE

Ringing the bell with a brave little air Marjorie waited. She recalled the first visit she had ever made to the president's house. On that occasion she had been a messenger for Miss Humphrey the registrar. That had been long ago, in her sophomore year. Since that day, her first personal meeting with President Matthews, Marjorie had become a welcome visitor and guest at Prexy's home. The maid, a stolid Swedish girl with pale gold hair and round blue eyes broke into smiles at sight of her.

"Gude afternoon, Miss Dean. How you ben all sommer?" she greeted Marjorie with pleased effusion.

"Good afternoon, Hilda. How have you been? I have been very well, and very happy."

"Tha's gude. I am pritty gude, too. We go sea shore, you know. Nize place. I go tak the bathe in the oshin. I gat awful much sunburn. Ha, ha!" Hilda showed her white teeth enjoyingly over her calamity. "You come see Mrs. Matthews? She is gone away this afternoon. The president is here. May-bee you come see him?"

"I hope your sunburn is all well now." Marjorie smiled at the jolly pink and white maid. "Yes, I came to see President Matthews. Is he busy?"

"He see you." Hilda nodded confidently. "You come in, pleese, Miss Dean. I tell him." She ushered Marjorie into the colonial reception hall and disappeared into the room at the right, the president's office. She was back in an instant with: "The president pleese to see you, Miss Dean."

"Good afternoon, Miss Marjorie. This is a most unexpected pleasure." President Matthews met Marjorie at the door of his office and warmly shook her by the hand. She saw that he was alone in the office.

"Good afternoon, President Matthews. I am very glad to see you. Miss Susanna and I are coming to make a social call upon Mrs. Matthews and you as soon as you are fairly settled again after your summer away from the campus. I came today on business of my own. I hoped to find you here and not too busy to see me." Marjorie's color heightened a trifle as she made the frank statement.

"I am at your service, Miss Marjorie." The president bowed her into a chair in his courtly fashion and sat down opposite her in his own. "What can I do for you?"

"I will give you a direct answer, and explain things afterward." Marjorie raised candid eyes to those of the president. "I wish you would give Leslie Cairns an opportunity to return to Hamilton College, and earn the degree she forfeited when she was expelled from Hamilton."

A dead silence followed her straight-forward request. President Matthews regarded her with contemplative gravity.

When he spoke it was to say: "You astonish me. Still I am confident you realize the peculiarity of the request you have just made." He continued to regard Marjorie as though half curious to learn what strong motive had prompted her amazing plea for reinstatement of the girl who had despitefully used her.

"Yes, I understand fully how much I am asking of you. Can it be done for Miss Cairns?" Again she came directly to the point.

"You mean from the standpoint of my permission and that of the Board?" he interrogated with equal directness.

"Yes." Marjorie inclined her head in affirmation.

"Well," President Matthews paused briefly; "such a thing has never been done at Hamilton. I do not say that it could not be arranged. Let me ask you, Miss Marjorie, what I regard as a most pertinent question: Why should such a sweeping favor be granted Miss Cairns? She furnished in my opinion, the most glaring example of bad conduct of any Hamilton culprit with whom I have ever had occasion to deal. However, I know you would not be here today with such a request except under strong conviction of right." He paused again, looking at her as though inviting an explanation.

"Miss Cairns has undergone a great change of mind and heart, President Matthews. I should like to tell you as much as I know of it," Marjorie returned. She was resolved to be frank, yet to choose her words so carefully as to spare Leslie so far as she could.

"I never knew Miss Cairns personally when she was a student at Hamilton," she began, "but last spring we became acquainted by chance." Marjorie thus magnanimously bridged over her years at Hamilton which Leslie Cairns had made so troublous for her.

Followed the interesting story of Peter Carden who had run away from Carden Hedge and made a name in finance for himself as Peter Cairns. She felt the intensity of President Matthews' interest as she continued to tell of Leslie's humiliating business mistake of having paid sixty thousand dollars for a garage site, the ground of which had already belonged to her father. Again Marjorie omitted all reference to the intended spitefulness of Leslie's business venture as in relation to the Travelers' dormitory enterprise. Nor was she to learn until long afterward that President Matthews had been in possession of the true state of Page and Dean's dormitory set-backs at the time when she made her earnest plea for Leslie.

Generously ignoring the past Marjorie chose to dwell instead upon Leslie's great affection for her father and of her desire for re-instatement at Hamilton solely on his account.

"I came to you upon my own responsibility, and unbeknown to Miss Cairns. Miss Susanna Hamilton and six of my best friends know this. Last night we met informally at Wayland Hall and discussed the matter. We are ready to help Miss Cairns in any way that we can should she be permitted to return to Hamilton. When she told me, on the way home from California, about her call upon you, I felt that she had not done herself justice. You were not in possession of the real facts of why she wished to come back to Hamilton. She could not put them before you as I could. So I am here." Her smile of kindly resolution was very beautiful.

"I am regarding Miss Cairns in a more favorable light; far more favorable than I had ever expected to regard her," the president admitted slowly.

"Oh, I forgot to mention one very important point," Marjorie added. "I have talked with Miss Remson about Miss Cairns. I know her to be great-spirited. She wishes to help Leslie."

"My own belief," came the hearty reply. "After all, Miss Marjorie, the burden of Miss Cairns' offenses were against yourself, Miss Remson and myself." The president smiled rather wryly. "You have chosen to eliminate yourself in the problem. I can do no better than to emulate your fine example of true Christian spirit. It remains for Miss Remson to speak her mind. In confidence I will say that the personal side of Miss Remson's and my grievances against Miss Cairns were never brought before the Board. Miss Cairns was expelled from Hamilton College together with her student confederates for hazing—and nothing other than hazing."

"Oh!" Marjorie could not repress the quick anxious ejaculation. She was suddenly seeing a dim light of hope, very faint, but a light, nevertheless.

The man saw the flash of hopeful eagerness spring into her face. His next speech was even more reassuring.

"You know how bitterly I am opposed to hazing," he said. "My attitude toward the students who were expelled from Hamilton for hazing you was implacable. It was perhaps more severe than that of my colleagues. A plea to the Board on my part for re-instatement for Miss Cairns may meet with success. I will call a meeting of the members soon. Considerable time has elapsed since the affair. Your wish in the matter——"

"Pardon me. Must my name be mentioned?" Marjorie questioned in a tone of dismay.

"Yes, since you wish to help Miss Cairns. It will be one of my strongest arguments in favor of re-instatement. While her desire to return to college because of regard for her father is commendable, this, in itself, may not impress the Board members. They may maintain that she should have thought of her duty to her father before she defied the rules of the college."

"If they could only know what such a re-instatement would mean to her!" was Marjorie's involuntary exclamation. "There is her side of it too. It is the side I intended to present to you in case you had not been in sympathy with me," she added naively.

"Indeed?" President Matthews regarded her with interested, half-amused eyes. He was thoroughly admiring her invincible spirit. "Will you tell me Miss Cairns' side of it?" he requested gently.

"Can you imagine anything harder than for Miss Cairns to re-enter Hamilton College under a cloud?" Marjorie's voice rang with appealing earnestness. "Her story is well known on the campus even though many of the students who were at Hamilton when she was there have been graduated. The Travelers will stand by her and try to make other students understand and respect her motive, should she be permitted to return. But she will undoubtedly be subjected to many humiliations. It will be a question of ethics, and there are so many different codes." Marjorie made a gesture expressive of futility. "Could she choose a thornier path of restitution?"

"True enough." The doctor bowed agreement. "It is you, rather than I, who should put Miss Cairns' case before the Board," he said, half smiling. "You have the courage of your convictions."

"Oh, no!" Marjorie looked her alarm. "I beg your pardon," she apologized in the same breath. "I didn't mean—I meant—" She stopped, rosy with confusion. "I am sure no one else could explain Leslie's case to the Board as you could, Dr. Matthews," she rallied with confidence. "It was easy for me to come to you because you are my friend. I would go before the Board, in order to help Leslie, if there were no other way open for me to do. But I should not like to do so." Her sunny smile flashed out with the confession.

"I understand your attitude in the matter, better, perhaps, than you may guess. I shall respect it, and try to present Miss Cairns' case to the Board members as sympathetically as you have presented it to me." The president answered her smile, his grave features lighting.

Marjorie breathed again at the reassurance. She was recalling the one occasion on which she has appeared before the Board. It had had strictly to do with expelling Leslie Cairns from Hamilton College. She was glad to remember now that her testimony then had added no weight to the evidence against Leslie.

"You underestimate your own powers, Miss Marjorie." She came back from remembrance of that dark day to hear the president saying. "Of all persons whom I know you have the best right to ask of and receive from the executives of Hamilton College the concession which you ask. You have accomplished for Hamilton that which I believe no one else could have done."

CHAPTER XI.

COMING BACK

"Well, Bean, beneficent, belated Bean, I thought you were never coming." Jerry Macy cheerfully addressed Marjorie from the top step of the veranda of Wayland Hall on which she was sitting viewing her chums' progress up the walk with an encouraging grin.

"It's only ten minutes past five," Marjorie defended, her eyes seeking the clock tower of Hamilton Hall.

"You said five o'clock," Jerry rebukingly reminded. "Learn to be dependable, my dear young lady. Then everyone will like you. I like you, anyway." Jerry favored Marjorie with an effulgent smile.

"Thank you so much," Marjorie bowed mock gratitude of Jerry's graciousness. "What are you doing out here all by yourself? Where is everyone?"

"I might say that I left the 'madding crowd' to watch for you. Alas, it would not be true!" Jerry sighed. "Nobody's home," she added in a practical tone. "Can you beat that?"

"Where is everybody?" Marjorie mounted the steps and dropped gracefully down beside Jerry.

"Scattered to the four winds. Miss Remson went to town and Ronny and Muriel went with her. Leila and Vera are off and away, whereabouts unknown. The two freshies who are to have Number arrived in a taxi about an hour ago. I assisted them with their luggage in my grandest post-graduate manner. They're still roosting in , and getting accustomed to the scenery. Where's Luciferous? I thought she'd be with you."

"She wasn't at Prexy's house. He was splendid, Jeremiah. He will do all he can for Leslie." Marjorie began an account of her interview with President Matthews.

"What do you know about that? What do you suppose she will say when she hears the good word?" Jerry looked pleased in spite of her none too warm regard for Leslie Cairns. "How do you suppose it will come to her? I wonder if Prexy will send for her to come to his office or if the Board will send her a notice, or what will happen?"

"I don't know. I'm wondering most of all when it will be. Prexy said he should call a Board meeting soon. Do you think I ought to tell Leslie what I've done?" Marjorie eyed Jerry with thoughtful anxiety. "It's almost certain."

Her color deepened as she thought of the president's words of earnest commendation.

"No, I don't." Jerry's answer was decided. "A surprise is one thing but a disappointment is quite another. I suppose she will live at the Hamilton House with Mrs. Gaylord. It seems queer to me—that our precious Hob-goblin, should be coming back to Hamilton as our bosom friend. It's high time we wound up our campus affairs, Marvelous Manager, and kept time to the wedding march."

"*We?* What *do* you mean, Jeremiah Macy?" Marjorie turned with merry suspicion upon Jerry.

"Nothing at all. I merely used 'we' as a figure of speech." Jerry's expression of innocence was perfect. The rush of tell-tale color to her cheeks betrayed her.

"You are an old fraud. You're going to marry Danny Seabrooke. You can't deny it." Marjorie shook a playful finger at Jerry.

"Bean, I cannot tell a lie. I am; someday. But not for a whole year. The engagement won't be announced till after your wedding. No one but Danny and the Macys and you know it. Swear, Marjorie Dean, that you won't——"

Jerry broke off abruptly. She sprang up and ran down the steps calling "Come along" over one plump shoulder. Approaching across the campus and within a few hundred yards of Wayland Hall she had spied three white-clad figures. Jerry made for the trio at a run, twirling a welcoming arm high above her head.

Marjorie rose hurriedly and followed Jerry in her jubilant dash, her radiant face showing her delight in beholding the newcomers.

"Robin Page! Dear precious Pagey!" she cried, holding out both arms to her tried and trusted partner of campus enterprise. "I nearly looked my eyes out coming across the campus this afternoon, hoping that three girls I saw getting out of a taxi at Silverton Hall were you and Phil and Barbara. They weren't. I was so disappointed."

"We arrived in the usual taxi not more than half an hour ago. Silverton Hall is filling up fast with aspiring freshmen. We didn't wait to make their acquaintance. Instead we started for Wayland Hall. We 'phoned the Arms first. Miss Susanna said you would be here at five."

Robin delivered this information between the enthusiastic embraces of her pretty partner. Page and Dean beamed at each other with utter good will. Then Jerry claimed Robin with a vigorous hug and kiss. Marjorie, Phyllis

Moore and Barbara Severn entwined arms in a triangular demonstration of buoyant affection.

"You should have seen us leave our luggage in one grand pyramid in the middle of Robin's room," laughed Phil Moore.

"Bags, suit cases, golf sticks, musical instruments, bundles, magazines and bandboxes all in reckless confusion," declared Barbara with a wave of the hand.

"We were crazy to see you. Where are the other girls? How about dinner at Baretti's?" Robin cried all in a breath.

"We've promised Miss Remson to stay here and spend the evening with her. You're respectfully invited to stick," Jerry told the welcome arrivals.

"All right. Guiseppe's tomorrow evening then," Robin returned radiantly.

"No; Hamilton Arms tomorrow evening. There's to be a Travelers' reunion," Marjorie interposed. "Kathie and Lillian will be home this evening. All the old Travelers except Helen Trent will be here then. And Phil and Barbara of the new ones. Helen is coming to visit us at the Arms in November. She'll stay till after Thanksgiving; maybe longer."

"Oh, lovely. It's simply glorious to be back." Robin drew a long rapturous breath. "The dormitory is progressing wonderfully. We made the taxi driver stop a moment today so that we could take a look at it."

"Mr. Graham says it will be ready for occupancy by the middle of March. Everything has gone as smoothly as could be this past summer, Robin. Mr. Graham says hardly an hour has been lost. He is making up daily for the time that was lost last winter. Things have gone ahead with such a rush since that set-back. The dormitory will be finished, he believes, not more than a month later than the date he first named for its completion."

"Isn't that glorious news?" Robin exclaimed animatedly. "Do you hear that, girls?" she called out to Phyllis and Barbara.

The reunited comrades were walking slowly toward the steps of the Hall now, arm in arm, their gay voices rising buoyantly on the stillness of the September afternoon. They had just reached the steps of the broad veranda when the throbbing of a taxicab engine brought all eyes to bear upon a station machine that was rolling up the drive.

"I hope it's the Bertramites," declared Marjorie.

"I choose to have it Doris Monroe," Jerry laughingly differed.

The Travelers had paused by common consent at the foot of the steps eagerly watching the nearing automobile.

"Good night!" broke from Jerry in a subdued, disgusted voice as she glimpsed the occupants of the taxicab through the now opened doorway of the machine. It had stopped on the graveled square before the house and the driver had sprung from his seat to open the rear door of the machine for his fares.

The expressions on both Marjorie's and Jerry's faces were unconscious indexes of their disappointment. Marjorie had been fondly hoping to see Augusta Forbes' tall graceful figure and handsome features emerge from the taxicab. Jerry knew that Muriel was most anxious for the return to the Hall of her roommate, Doris Monroe. To see moon-eyed Julia Peyton poke her head suspiciously out of the door of the machine had inspired Jerry with deep disgust.

The tall squarely-built figure of the sophomore who had stirred up so much trouble during the previous year followed the peering, pasty-white face and large round black eyes with their owl-like stare. Julia Peyton straightened, at the same time casting a darting glance at the group of girls near the steps. She drew her black brows together frowningly at sight of the quintette. With no sign of recognition she turned her back belligerently upon them and devoted herself to paying the driver.

Her companion of the taxicab, a short plump girl with a disagreeable face and bright red hair, emulated Julia's example, her nose elevated to a haughty angle.

With the air of a grenadier, Julia picked up a leather bag which she had set down on the graveled space while she paid the driver. She stalked toward the steps across the small graveled interval, her black eyes fastened upon the front doorway of the Hall.

"Good afternoon Miss Peyton," Marjorie greeted composedly as the haughty arrival passed the group. "Good afternoon, Miss Carter."

A combined murmur of greeting arose from the other four Travelers who were quick to follow Marjorie's lead.

Neither by word nor sign did Julia Peyton indicate that she was aware of the courteous salutation. Her chum and roommate, Clara Carter, imitated Julia in the discourtesy. The pair went grandly up the steps and to the door where Julia pressed a finger to the electric bell. Without waiting for a maid she flung open the screen door and stepped into the reception hall with Clara at her heels.

"A bad beginning makes a good ending. So 'tis said," Phil Moore commented with cheerful satire as the unsociable pair of arrivals disappeared into the house.

"A decidedly bad beginning I should say," Barbara Severn's shoulders lifted with a disapproving shrug. "How extremely silly to carry one's prejudices and resentments to such an extent."

"It certainly is. Just the same if Marjorie hadn't spoken to those two girls first, I shouldn't have," Robin confessed. "Not because of past displeasure toward them. It is one's first impulse to return such a discourtesy in kind."

"Did you imagine they would speak to you, Marjorie?" was Barbara's interested question.

Marjorie smilingly shook her head. "No," she said, "Miss Peyton hasn't spoken to me since the evening of the Rustic Romp last spring. She has been nice to Leila, though. And generally to you, Robin, hasn't she?"

"Um-m; so, so." Robin answered lightly. "She certainly didn't speak to me today."

"That was only because you were with me," Marjorie declared.

"And me," echoed Jerry. "Don't leave me out of things. There has been a Peyton-Macy feud ever since the night last year when Miss Peyton reported the social gathering in Fifteen as noisy, and she and I exchanged pleasantries. You three innocent, trusting Silvertonites were snubbed because of the company you keep."

"May we always be found in the same company," Robin said gaily.

"I wish we could all go up to Fifteen," Marjorie remarked half wistful. "Annie says she thinks it has been taken. She heard Miss Remson tell Leila yesterday that she was saving it for someone. It hadn't been taken, though, day before yesterday when I last saw Miss Remson."

"Oh, let's go into the living room then," Robin proposed. "I have stacks of business to transact with you, dear partner." She reached out and drew Marjorie into the circle of a loving arm. "Phil and Barby and Jerry can entertain one another."

"What sort of entertainment do you prefer?" Phil asked Jerry with polite solemnity.

"I don't know. I am not used to being entertained," giggled Jerry.

The quintette were animatedly mounting the steps, their merry voices and fresh, light-hearted laughter enlivening the vacation quiet which had hung over the hall during the long summer days in the absence of the Hamilton girls to whom it yearly gave canopy.

Barbara's keen ears were quick to catch the hum of an approaching motor. "Oh, there's another taxicab coming!" she called out. "This time let's hope it is Miss Remson and the girls."

A battery of expectant glances was turned upon the station taxicab as it sped up the drive toward the house. A concerted little shout of jubilation went up from the watchers as it stopped and Veronica stepped lightly from the machine followed by Miss Remson, whom she gallantly assisted to alight, and Muriel.

"Oh, frabjous day!" Muriel made a rush for the three returned Silvertonites. A joyful tumult ensued, during which the driver of the taxicab circled the laughing, chattering knot of women in an uneasy prance, anxious to collect his fares and be gone.

Through an open window of the long second-story hall the merry sounds of rejoicing floated to the ears of Julia Peyton, who had been conducting a tour of investigation up and down the hall for her own satisfaction. She went to the window which overlooked the front yard and drive. Standing well back from it she sourly watched the animated, laughing group gather on the gravelled space below. The instant she saw it begin to move toward the steps she darted away from the window and into her room.

"What's the matter?" Clara Carter had already removed her hat and traveling coat and was lounging in a cushioned wicker chair. She turned pale blue curious eyes upon Julia as the latter fairly dashed into the room, closing the door.

"Nothing is the matter, except that I don't choose to be out in the hall when that crowd of P. G.'s comes upstairs," she said crossly. "I've made up my mind to one thing. This year I am not going to have any more silly crushes like the one I had on Doris Monroe. I'm going to make the dramatic club and be of importance on the campus."

CHAPTER XII.

A MYSTERY ABOUT

"It's all right! It's all right! Oh, splendid, great, celostrous!"

Marjorie slipped from her chair at the breakfast table in the sun-lit morning room of Hamilton Arms and began a vigorously joyful dance around the room, waving a letter over her head, her lovely face aglow.

"Thank you for using my new adjective," Jerry commented politely, "but why such enthusiasm? Why such joyful gyrations?"

"Can't you guess? Take a look at that envelope by my plate and you'll know." Marjorie came back to the table and resumed her place.

"I know. But then, I am a better guesser than Jerry," Miss Susanna declared jokingly. "Your letter is from Doctor Matthews."

"How could I know? Prexy Matthews never writes letters to me," Jerry defended. "I'm neither a benefactor nor a biographer."

"Yes, it is from Prexy. Listen to what he writes." Marjorie read in an utterly happy tone:

> "DEAR MISS MARJORIE:
>
> "It becomes my great pleasure to inform you that I have successfully presented Miss Cairns' case to the Hamilton College Board. I took up the matter with the members at a special meeting which I called on the day after our conversation relative to the matter. They asked for three days' time in which to consider Miss Cairns' case.
>
> "Yesterday afternoon at a special meeting called by the chairman of the Board at Hamilton Hall the Board members came to the decision that, in the circumstances, Miss Cairns was to be commended in her desire toward moral restitution. Your plea in her behalf was incorporated into a regular motion which was voted upon. A unanimous vote in her favor was cast. It was also voted that I should notify Miss Cairns of her eligibility to return to Hamilton College as a student.
>
> "Relative to notifying Miss Cairns of the Board's favorable decision I should prefer to consult you in the matter before taking action. You may have some special preference in this respect which I should be glad to honor. Will you call at my

office in Hamilton Hall at your convenience, on any afternoon of the week before Saturday, and before four o'clock?

"Yours cordially,

"ROBERT EAMES MATTHEWS."

Miss Susanna rose, trotted from the head of the oblong table to the foot and put both arms about Marjorie's neck. "You good little thing," she said with half quavering tenderness. "You deserve all the happiness life can give you. You've given Leslie her surest chance of becoming what she hopes now to be."

"You would have done the same. I only happened to think of it first because she told me about having gone to Prexy herself," Marjorie sturdily refused to credit herself with having done anything worthy of laudation.

"That's the way all the big things for humanity have been done, child," Miss Susanna returned soberly. "Some wholly unselfish person has happened to think of the other fellow first. Happened to think because his or her mind was centered on doing good."

"You're so dear, Goldendede." Marjorie rubbed a soft cheek against Miss Susanna's encircling arm. She chose this method of wriggling gracefully away from praise. "I'm going to send Leslie a telegram this morning asking her to come to Hamilton at once. I'll go to see Prexy this very afternoon," she decided with her usual promptness.

"That's the right idea," Jerry commended. "How I wish I could do noble deeds like you, Bean. I haven't a single celostrous act to my credit that I know of. At least Miss Susanna hasn't praised me for any," she added. Her mischievous grin bespoke her lack of regret at her confessed defection.

"Nonsense." Miss Susanna's merry little chuckle was heard. "I'm surprised at your lack of conceit, Jeremiah. I know right now of three very celostrous acts to your credit."

"Name them," challenged Jerry. "Listen closely, Bean. Jeremiah is going to be praised. Ahem. All ready." She straightened in her chair, lifted her dimpled chin, and put on a fixed stare of expectant modesty.

"You helped Jonas take up and put away the dahlia tubers. He hates that job. Second. You planned every bit of the Santa Claus fun last Christmas on purpose for a crotchety old woman who had never known much about Santa when she was a lonely kiddie. Third. You are a never ending source of diversion to your friends and a joy to have in the house. If you don't believe that you are, go and ask Jonas," the old lady finished humorously.

"I wouldn't think of being so conceited." Jerry put one hand before her face and peered bashfully around it at Miss Susanna.

"I can add something to what Miss Susanna says." Marjorie's gaze rested fondly upon Jerry. "You are the best pal in the world, Jeremiah. You have——"

"No, I haven't. Excuse me. Good-bye. I'm going to help Jonas rake leaves this morning to put around the rose bushes. Want me to run you over to the campus in the car after luncheon?" she asked Marjorie as she reached the door.

"No, thank you. I'm going to walk. You'd better go with me, though. I am going to the Hall to see Miss Remson and the girls. I have an idea buzzing madly." Marjorie smilingly tapped one side of her curly head. "You can rally the Travelers in Ronny's room while I go to the Hall to see Prexy."

Jerry came back. She paused beside Marjorie, head bent toward Marjorie's curly one in an attitude of strained listening. "I can't hear it," she said.

"You're going to, since you've taken the trouble to come back to listen for it. I was going to tell you, anyway. We ought to initiate Leslie Cairns into the Travelers on the same day she hears the good news from Prexy." Marjorie glanced inquiringly from Jerry to Miss Hamilton. "We'd have a funny initiation for her; like the one we conducted for Phil and Barbara. It would put her at ease with us."

"A good idea," Miss Susanna instantly approved.

"You bet it is," Jerry echoed with slangy emphasis. "But for goodness' sake let us have it in Muriel's room. It's farthest away from the retreat of the Screech Owl and the Phonograph. Let's give them no chance this time to complain of noise on our part."

"We'll invite the Lady of the Arms and the Empress of Wayland Hall to the initiation, then they won't dare complain," Marjorie laughed. "Too bad we can't have it in good old . It's larger than either Ronny's or Muriel's room."

"Has someone taken ?" Jerry asked quickly. "I forgot to ask you about it when you came from the Hall last time."

"Miss Remson said the other day that she was considering a student who might take it. She seemed rather indefinite about it, so I didn't ask her any further questions. Will you come to Leslie's initiation, Miss Susanna?"

In spite of Marjorie's merry assertion that the Lady of the Arms would be present on the gala occasion she now turned to the mistress of the Arms with the pretty deference which she had ever accorded Miss Susanna since their first meeting.

"Thank you, Marvelous Manager. I shall be delighted to attend such a splendid demonstration of your marvelous managing," was the old lady's indulgent reply.

"And we shall be even more delighted to have you." Marjorie rose from her chair and offered a gay arm to her hostess. "Let me escort you into the sitting room, dear Goldendede."

"No; let me." Jerry offered the other arm.

The three paraded out of the morning room and down the wide, old-fashioned center hall to the sitting room.

"You'd better hurry up if you expect to rake any leaves today," was Jonas's succinct advice to Jerry as he appeared in the hall in overalls to consult Miss Susanna about certain of her rose bushes. "I'll have 'em all raked up myself before you get near 'em."

This warning, which was Jonas's favorite method of joking sent Jerry's gallantry to the winds. She dropped Miss Susanna's arm and fled for the tool house and a rake.

After spending an hour with Miss Hamilton in the sitting room Marjorie went up stairs to the study. There, with Brooke Hamilton's deep-blue eyes upon her, she wrote her semi-weekly letter to Hal. She loved best to write to him in the quietness and peace of the room where she had learned the truth of her love for him because of Brooke Hamilton's disappointment and sorrow.

"I am going to work on your story again before long," she whimsically promised the portrait of the founder of Hamilton College as she settled herself at the antique library table to write to Hal. "I haven't forgotten you, but for a while I must leave you and work for your college."

It was with a feeling of glad exultation which brought a starry brightness to her eyes and a deeper tide of rose to her cheeks that she left Jerry at Wayland Hall after luncheon and went on with a springy, happy step to stately Hamilton Hall. She had already telephoned a telegram to the telegraph office in the town of Hamilton. The telegram was to Leslie, at her apartment in Central Park West, New York City. She had confidently worded it: "Come to Hamilton at once. Important. Wire day and train. Marjorie."

Her interview with President Matthews was brief but eminently satisfactory. It resulted in the arrangement that on whatever day Leslie Cairns should arrive in Hamilton she should be escorted to President Matthews' office by Marjorie, there to hear the good news from the head of the college himself.

As she went down the steps of Hamilton Hall she had hard work to keep from setting off across the campus at a frisky run. She decided with a smile dimpling the corners of her red lips that the dignity of the occasion forbade it. When within a few yards of the Hall, however, dignity ceased to count. She sped high-heartedly across the short thick campus grass to the steps, intent only upon seeing her chums and laying her kindly plan before them.

"You had better make up your mind to stay here to dinner this evening, children," Miss Remson offered this advice to Marjorie and Jerry shortly after Marjorie's arrival. To the great disappointment of both girls not one of the Wayland Hall Travelers was at home. "Call up the other Travelers and tell them to come, too. Then you can go into your old room, , and discuss the initiation of Leslie Cairns. I must say it is the very last thing I should suppose might happen." The little manager's tone was one of accepted wonder at such a state of affairs.

"Hasn't been taken yet?" Jerry cannily fished for information.

"Not yet." Jerry surprised an odd, wise, bird-like gleam in the little manager's kindly eyes which she knew of old to mean that Miss Remson had a secret she was shrewdly guarding. "A senior I know has the refusal of it. She has not decided upon it yet. I had two applications yesterday for it. I wish you and Marjorie were to have it this year. Now girls, go and do your telephoning. I must see the cook about the dinner." Miss Remson bustled off in her alert, brisk manner.

"There's some kind of mystery afoot about old ," Jerry surmised shrewdly. "You can't fool Jeremiah. She has what Leila calls 'the seeing eye.' I can see all right enough that Miss Remson has something on *her* mind about our old fond, familiar hanging-out place that she isn't ready to tell us. When she does get ready to talk about it, it will be some surprise, Bean; some surprise."

CHAPTER XIII.

UNDER THE BIG ELM

"Am I awake, or dreaming? Did I come out of Hamilton Hall just now? If I did, what was it I heard Prexy say? Prexy." Leslie Cairns repeated the name with tremulous satisfaction. "I've a right to say it now. Thanks to *you*, Marjorie Dean, I am back on the campus again. I'm going to cry, Marjorie. I was determined I wouldn't before Prexy. I tried to take my pardon like a good soldier. But now I am thinking of my father. What will Peter the Great say?"

"I think Peter the Great will say, 'Go to it, Cairns II., and be the happiest person I know.'" Marjorie assured, smiling her amusement of Leslie's reference to her father as Peter the Great. "Come on over to the Bean holder, Leslie. We can sit there for awhile, and, if you must cry, no one will notice your weeps."

Her arm tucked into one of Leslie Cairns', Marjorie began steering her companion gently toward a great-trunked, towering elm tree some distance east of Hamilton Hall under which were two rustic benches.

"This is my favorite tree on the campus, Leslie," Marjorie introduced her companion to the giant campus sentinel with a cheery wave of the hand. "You named me Bean, and the girls named this seat the Bean holder because I've always loved to come here." All this with a view toward dispelling Leslie's desire to cry.

That which Leslie had believed could never come to pass had happened. She and Marjorie Dean had just emerged from Hamilton Hall where she had gone with Marjorie a brief twenty minutes before to hear from President Matthews the amazing news of her re-instatement as a student at Hamilton College.

"That wretched name, Bean. It makes me laugh." Leslie was half laughing, half crying. "It always made me laugh, even when I thought I hated you."

"It's a fine name. I'm awfully fond of it," Marjorie assured with sunny good humor.

They made the rest of the short journey to the seat under the big elm in silence. Leslie continued to fight desperately against shedding tears. Marjorie was sympathetically leaving her to herself until she should recover her usual amount of poise.

"The view of the campus is beautiful from here," Marjorie said as they seated themselves on one of the two benches drawn up near the tree. She looked off across the expanse of living green, worship of her old friend, the campus, in her wide brown eyes.

Leslie assented. Her gaze was directed to Marjorie rather than the campus. She thought she had never seen anyone quite so lovely. Today Marjorie had blossomed out in the pale jade frock of softest silk and black fur trimmings which Jerry had advocated on the occasion of her first call upon President Matthews. From the crown of the small hat which matched her frock to the dainty narrowness of her black satin slippers Marjorie was a delight to the eyes.

Attired in a two-piece traveling frock of distinctive English weave and make, Leslie herself was looking far more attractive than in the old days when she had been a student at Hamilton. Happiness and a clear conscience had done much to change her former lowering, disagreeable facial expression to one of pleasant alertness and good humor. She had come to Hamilton the day following the receipt of Marjorie's telegram on an early afternoon train, Marjorie had met her at the station and after a luncheon at the Ivy the two girls had gone direct to Hamilton Hall.

Now that Leslie was in possession of the glad knowledge that her dearest wish had been granted Marjorie had other plans for her of which she was totally unaware as she sat staring half absently at the campus, her mind busy with wondering what her father would say when he heard the blessed news she had to tell him.

"I'll go back to New York tomorrow, Marjorie, and tell Peter the Great the good news. Then I'll give Mrs. Gaylord three times a year's salary and have my father book passage for her to Europe on the Monarch. She's crazy to go to England and France. I shan't need her. I'm going to engage board in one of the off-campus boarding houses." Leslie broke the silence with this decided announcement. "I could live at the Hamilton House with Mrs. Gaylord as a chaperon, but I'd rather not. I'd be too conspicuous. Of course, I'd love to live in one of the campus houses. But that's out of the question."

"I wish you could live on the campus, Leslie. I think it would be best for you, if you could find a vacancy. It's almost too late now to hope to find one. I'll inquire tomorrow for you, and see what I can learn." Marjorie spoke with the utmost friendly concern.

"No; don't." Leslie shook a vigorous head. "There's not a manager of a campus house who doesn't know my record when I was here before. Not one of them would consent to take me. Besides"—Leslie hesitated—"there's only one house on the campus where I'd care to live—Wayland Hall. That's out of the question. You can understand why." A flush of shame mounted to Leslie's cheeks.

"It wouldn't be if there were a vacancy at the Hall," Marjorie declared. "Miss Remson is glad you are to come back to Hamilton. She knows about it. I told her the other day after receiving Prexy's letter. Our old room, Fifteen, was vacant when I first came back. If I had been sure of succeeding with Prexy and the Board for you, I would have asked Miss Remson to save Fifteen for you. But I wasn't sure. Besides, I couldn't know what your plans might be, in case I should succeed."

"I'd never go back to the Hall after the way I made trouble for Miss Remson," Leslie replied with gloomy positiveness. "No; I'll find as good a boarding house as I can off the campus. Understand, Marjorie, I'd rather live on the campus for one big reason. I'd have to fight to live down my past record as a snob and a trouble-maker. That would be good for me, though. I'd be gossiped about; maybe ostracized by a large proportion of the students. But I'd work as hard for democracy as I'd once worked against it. And the Travelers would stand by me. Perhaps before next Commencement I'd have come into a better light in the eyes of the Hamilton crowd, students and faculty."

She paused, then shrugged her shapely shoulders and continued with a short laugh: "Forget it. That's only a day dream I've been indulging myself in. You see I keep thinking of trying to square myself on the campus because of Peter the Great. I want him to come and live at Carden Hedge, and be happy. I'd love to have the Leila Harper Playhouse presented to Leila by him. So I soar off into splendid schemes of how I can make good at Hamilton and bring everything out lovely like the end of a fairy tale. It can't be done, Bean." Leslie used the nickname with absent affection.

"There is one thing I can do," she went on in a tone of purposeful energy. "I can complete my college course and win my sheepskin. You've made that opportunity possible for me. I hope I can some day do something for you to show my appreciation, Marjorie."

"You can. This very afternoon." Marjorie had been wondering how she might find means to persuade Leslie to go to Wayland Hall with her. She was confident that Leslie would refuse the invitation which she was awaiting a favorable moment to extend. She seized upon her companion's grateful declaration with dancing eyes. "You can come over to Wayland Hall with me. I'm going to meet Jerry there. Come on." Marjorie had risen from the seat and was holding out an inviting hand to Leslie.

"Oh, I—" Leslie checked herself and stood up. "All right," she agreed cheerfully. In the face of her recent serious assertion she was determined not to flinch.

Marjorie cast a furtive glance at her wrist watch as she drew one of Leslie's arms within her own. It was exactly 4 o'clock. The two girls headed across the campus for the Hall. Leslie scanned the veranda of the house where she had once courted and met disaster with anxious eyes. She was relieved to see not a girl in sight. Marjorie was also watching the veranda for a very different reason.

They were within a short distance of the Hall when a girl in a sleeveless apricot frock came out on the veranda. She spied the pair and twirled a plump bare arm above her head, disappearing inside in a hurry.

"There's Jerry." The dancing lights strengthened in Marjorie's brown eyes. "She's watching for us." Tightening her light hold upon her companion's arm she hastily escorted her up the steps and to the door. It opened suddenly. Three pairs of arms reached forth from across the threshold, seized Leslie and hustled her into the house. Next instant she stood bewildered, but smiling, in the hall surrounded by a merry group of girls. Her initiation in the Travelers had begun.

CHAPTER XIV.

AN AMBITIOUS PLAN

Two hours later Leslie Cairns had been initiated into the Travelers' jolly sorority and had acquitted herself with credit. She had done herself proud in the cream-puff eating test, which consisted of blindfolding the victim and giving her a cream puff to eat from her hands. She had nobly pushed the required penny over the floor with her nose, she had drunk a cup of deadly poison urged upon her by her initiators which had turned out to be very strong sage tea, and she had performed other ridiculously difficult stunts with giggling zest and finish.

By the time the dinner bell rang Leslie was feeling more at home with the bevy of girls she had once scorned than she had ever dreamed she might. With the exception of Helen Trent the original eleven Travelers were present. Since their particular initial sorority had been enlarged to nineteen members Leslie had been received into it as the twentieth member. This meant the second chapter to which Phil and Barbara belonged might also have the privilege of electing a twentieth member to their chapter. The new chapter chosen the previous June were also in line for a twentieth member.

Neither by word nor sign had the merry party of girls shown themselves to be aware of the fact that Leslie was returning to Hamilton under unusual circumstances. Everything was ignored save that she was an honored candidate for admission into the Travelers' sorority.

Despite the fact that Room was to pass into the possession of a mysterious senior who might appear at any time to claim it, Miss Remson had urged the Travelers to make it their initiation headquarters. This time there had been no hanging of heavy curtains over the doors of the room. The preponderance of the students to reside at Wayland Hall had not yet arrived on the campus. There was therefore small possibility of anyone being disturbed by the merry-making in Fifteen.

In honor of the occasion the Wayland Hall Travelers had converted one of the couch beds into a throne such as had been erected on a previous occasion when Miss Susanna Hamilton had first visited Marjorie in her room at the Hall and been introduced to Miss Remson.

The middle place upon the throne had been reserved for Leslie. She had been impressively informed that, when she should have courageously passed through the terrible ordeal ahead of her, she would then be eligible to the middle place on the throne. Miss Susanna Hamilton and Miss Remson occupied the seats on the right and left of the glorified dais, looking like a pair of small bright-eyed birds in full plumage.

Marjorie had fondly ordered the party to be a dress affair. In consequence Miss Remson was resplendent in a ravishing gray satin gown which Leila had brought from Europe as a present to her old friend. Miss Susanna had on the wisteria satin gown which she had worn at Castle Dean on the previous Christmas day. The Travelers had decked themselves in their prettiest afternoon frocks. They resembled a flock of bright-hued butterflies which had suddenly made pause in Marjorie's and Jerry's old-time haunt before resuming their flight.

When the gay revelers trooped down to dinner, which was to be served to them at a special long table, the attention of the few students in the dining-room immediately became riveted upon the merry little company. Besides themselves there were eight other girls in the dining-room. Of these eight only two pairs of eyes were directed in good-natured amusement at the vivacious table full of girls. The other six pairs held a variety of expressions running from curiosity to dark envy.

"Catch Miss Remson allowing us to have any such noisy party," Julia Peyton muttered jealously to Clara Carter as the two girls left the dining room. A rippling burst of laughter from the guest table further fanned the displeasure that flamed in Julia's breast against the merry diners. She was particularly incensed at seeing Leslie Cairns among them.

"Miss Dean and Miss Macy must have come back to the Hall again. That's the reason for the pow-wow they've been having in ," Clara Carter surmised as they started up the stairs. "That little old woman in lavender must be Miss Remson's sister. One is about as homely as the other. It's queer, though, about that Miss Cairns being with them."

"Very queer; *altogether too queer*," was Julia's bitter retort. "She has no right to be here at the Hall. If she comes here again I shall make an objection to Miss Remson. She's an expelled student. Besides the way she sneaked into the gym under cover of a mask at thc Romp was simply outrageous. I can't understand how Miss Remson can overlook such things."

"I heard that she lived at Wayland Hall until she was expelled and that her father was a multi-millionaire. Probably Miss Remson has a healthy respect for her father's money. Maybe she is visiting Miss Remson. If she is, you can't say a word." Clara pointed out sagely.

A baffled expression crossed Julia's frowning features. "It won't take me long to find out what she is doing here," she sullenly boasted. "She is entirely to blame for my falling-out with Doris. It was over her Doris and I disagreed. I hope Doris will someday understand that I only tried to be her friend in warning her against Miss Cairns."

"Doris Monroe is a very selfish girl. I don't intend to bother being nice to her at all this year," Clara declared, pursing her lips in disapproval.

"Don't be alarmed. She won't bother herself about you, or me, either," Julia threw open the door of their room and stalked into it. She flung herself sulkily into a chair, her pale, moon-eyed face full of vengeful spleen. "I detest that hateful crowd of P.G.'s!" she exclaimed. "They do precisely as they please, here. We other students have no rights. What good does it do to assert oneself to Miss Remson? She is hand in glove with them."

"I think it would be a good idea for us to change houses," was Clara's meditative suggestion. She had seated herself in a chair opposite Julia with an air of great wisdom. "It's not too late to engage board somewhere else on the campus."

"What are you talking about?" Julia turned a contemptuous gaze upon her chum. "I'll say there is not a vacancy on the campus by now."

"Well, we could find a couple of girls who would be glad to exchange houses with us. Wayland Hall is considered the best house on the campus." There was crafty method in Clara's suggestion. Secretly she had no desire to leave the Hall. Knowing Julia's stubborn contrariness she had but to propose making a change in order to clinch her roommate's determination not to do so.

"You are correct in saying it's the best house on the campus. When you see me leaving it because of a crowd of girls like the one down stairs, you will see something startling. Last year I endured a great deal of unfairness rather than be continually making complaints. This year I shall do differently. I intend to begin this very evening," Julia announced with belligerent decision.

"What are you going to do?" Clara focussed eager attention upon her companion. In spite of hers and Julia's frequent disagreements she could be relied upon to do battle under Julia's banner.

"I'm going to unpack my traveling bag, first of all." Julia rose with a sudden burst of combative energy. "If those girls begin to be noisy when they come up stairs I shall go straight down stairs to Miss Remson and demand that she does something about it."

"Suppose she should be upstairs with them? You know yourself that she was up there a long time before dinner. And her sister was with her." Clara had kept a vigilant watch upon the movements of the company in through a discreetly narrow opening in their own door.

"Then I shall reprimand her before the whole crowd in for not keeping better order in the house."

"You wouldn't dare do that?" Clara challenged in a half admiring tone.

"Oh, yes, I should. Who is Miss Remson? A manager. Well, what is a manager but an upper servant? I'd certainly not be afraid to speak my mind to our housekeeper at home. That's all Miss Remson is. What she needs is to be told her place, and be made to keep it."

"I've often thought the same thing," Clara refused to be subservient to Julia in opinion. "Did you notice the other students in the dining room tonight?" she asked with a knowing glance toward Julia.

"No. What about them?" Julia paused in the midst of her unpacking to look sharply at her Titian-haired roommate.

"Every single one of them acted as though they didn't think much of that P. G. crowd. I kept watch of them. It seems to me," Clara tilted her flame-colored head to one side, a sure indication that she was planning mischief, "that it would be a pretty good plan for us to start a crowd of our own this year at the Hall. If we could count on as many as half of the students at the Hall to stand by us, we could make Miss Remson play fairly with us. She'd not dare favor that one crowd above us."

"That's a good idea." Julia looked impressed. She turned from laying out her belongings on the study table and leaned against it, eyeing Clara speculatively. She began counting on her fingers: "One, two, three, four, five of those Bertram students. Then there are Miss Harper and Miss Mason; seven. Five of the Sanford P. G. crowd; twelve. Doris Monroe makes thirteen. Of course a few other students in the house will stick to them. Not more than six or seven at most. Gussie Forbes isn't popular in this house except with the Sanford and Bertram crowds. You know the sophs at the Hall voted against her at the election of class officers last fall."

"But they voted for Doris Monroe," Clara reminded with a frown, "and now Doris has gone over to the P. G. crowd."

"Yes, and she is not going to gain a thing by it, either," was Julia's satisfied prophesy. "Most of the sophs who voted for Doris don't like Miss Dean and her pals. They can't stand the calm way those girls have of trying to be the whole thing, and run everything. Annie told me today that there were to be nine new students at the Hall, all freshies but one. Those girls we saw tonight in the dining room must be freshies. Tomorrow we'll make it a point to get acquainted with the freshies. It's really our duty as upper classmen."

"Yes, indeed," echoed Clara. "By the time Doris Monroe comes back we may have our own crowd well started. We might form a sorority." Her mechanical tones, which Muriel and Jerry had naughtily compared to a phonograph, rose exultantly. "You could be the president of it," she accorded magnanimously, "and I would be the vice-president. We could get up a really exclusive, social club and entertain a lot—and be popular." Her pal's eyes gleamed at the prospect of popularity. It was the dream of both girls to enjoy a popularity on the campus equal to if not greater than that of Doris Monroe, though neither possessed any of the necessary requisites.

"We'll do it. We can get up a better sorority than that old Travelers' club, and not half try," Julia predicted with supreme egotism. "This is the way we'll do. We'll wait until the Hall is full, then we'll select the girls here that we want for the club and send them an invitation to a luncheon at the Ivy. We'll have very handsome engraved invitations, and I'll preside at the luncheon. After we have the sorority well-started we can give plays and shows just for amusement. We shan't try to make money. Leave that to those beggarly Travelers. We'll make our entertainments strictly invitation affairs. Miss Dean and her crowd have simply ruined the social atmosphere of Hamilton by welfare experiments. The object of our club shall be to restore it. Let me tell you we'll have plenty of sympathizers. Just wait. Doris Monroe will be very sorry yet that she didn't stick to us."

CHAPTER XV.

THE MYSTERIOUS SENIOR

Blissfully unaware of Julia Peyton's ambitious schemes against them and democracy at Hamilton the Travelers finished their dessert amidst plenty of fun and laughter and flocked upstairs and into again, there to spend one of their old-time merry "stunt" evenings.

Ronny danced to Phil's violin music. Robin sang, accompanied by the same talented, infallible musician. Phil's violin playing had become institutional with the Travelers. She was always equal to musical emergency. Leila and Vera convulsed their buoyant audience with a quaintly humorous Irish dialogue which they had found in an old book while in Ireland and had gleefully learned. Jerry partly sang a popular song off the key until she was drowned out by laughter.

Muriel recited a monologue which she had composed and named: "Back on the campus." Barbara sang a French song. Kathie and Lillian endeavored to sing together an old German song precisely as Professor Wenderblatt was wont to sing it in his full bass voice. They broke down in the midst of deep-uttered bass growls and gutterals and lost track of the tune so completely they never found it again, but subsided with laughter.

Marjorie and Lucy pleaded having no stunt to offer and were each ordered to recite their favorite short poem. Marjorie thereupon recited "To a Grecian Urn," and Lucy gave Poe's weird, "Ulalume." Leslie won quick approval by her prompt response to the demand by giving a funny series of imitations.

The feature of the stunt party was contributed, however, by Miss Remson and Miss Susanna. They had conducted a chuckling confab together at one end of the room into which they had invited Phil. She had listened to them, then laughingly nodded, played a few bars of an odd little tune on her violin and returned to her place in the center of the room.

When Phil presently tapped on her violin with her bow, the two little old ladies stepped gaily out, hand in hand, in a lively jigging dance. They pranced forward and back, clasped right hands above their heads and jigged around each other, clasped left hands and jigged again, joined right and left hands and spun in a circle then polkaed up and down the room with spirit. There were other variations to the dance which they performed with equal sprightliness. Their delighted audience gurgled and squealed with laughter, breaking forth into riotous applause as the jigging pair reached their throne and sank upon their cushions, breathless and laughing.

Marjorie thought she had never seen a prettier sight than the pair of dainty little old ladies in their charming satin dresses stepping out so blithely to the old-fashioned polka.

"That is the Glendon Polka if you care to know it," Miss Susanna informed the girls. "I used to dance it as a girl, and I found that the Empress of Wayland Hall knew how to dance it, too. I learned to dance it before going to my first party. Uncle Brooke engaged a dancing master to come and teach me the latest dances."

"The latest dances." Jerry said with an enjoying chuckle. "Not much like a fox trot, is it?"

"I believe I must have learned that polka from the same dancing master," Miss Remson said. "I lived in West Hamilton as a girl and went to dancing school. It was a Professor Griggs who taught me the Glendon polka."

"The same man," Miss Susanna declared brightly. The two old ladies beamed at each other. This little coincidence relative to their youth served to strengthen the bond of friendship between them.

"This is the queer part of the Glendon polka," Phil said. "When Miss Susanna said she and Miss Remson were going to do an old-time dance called the Glendon polka, I remembered I'd seen that title in an old music book at home. I had tried it and learned to play it when I first began to take violin lessons as a kiddie. I had liked it because it was such a frisky little tune."

"You never dreamed then that someday you would play it for two old ladies to frisk to, did you?" Miss Remson gently pinched Phil's cheek as she sat balanced on the edge of the throne, her violin in hand.

"I never did," Phil laughed. "I'll never forget the Glendon polka."

"It seems we hadn't forgotten how to dance it in spite of our years," Miss Susanna said with a little nod of satisfaction.

"Did you know there were prizes to be given for the best stunts?" Katherine Langly joined the group around the throne. Kathie was looking her radiant best in a coral beaded afternoon frock of Georgette. Her blue eyes were sparkling with light and life and her red lips broke readily into smiles. She bore small likeness to the sad, self-effacing sophomore the Travelers had taken under their protective wing at the beginning of their freshman year at Hamilton. Kathie was now commencing her second year as a member of the faculty. She was famed on the campus as a playwright and her triumphantly literary future was assured. She had already sold several short stories to important magazines and had begun her first novel.

"Ronny is going to be magnificently generous, so she says, and give out the prizes. She's gone to her room after them," Lillian added to the information Kathie had just given.

"'Magnificently generous'" Kathie repeated suspiciously. "That doesn't sound promising to me. I know she means us."

"Could any persons be more worthy of a prize," giggled Lillian. "Remember how hard we worked."

Ronny soon returned wearing a mischievous expression. She carried a good-sized paper-wrapped package on one arm. In one hand she held two small packages which suggested jewelry. The girls guessed the large bundle to contain one or more boxes of the delicious candied fruit from her ranch home of which she always had a stock on hand.

"Hear, hear!" Ronny placed her bundles on the table and waved both arms above her head for attention. "Who had the best stunt?" she called out. "Altogether; answer!"

"The Lady of the Arms and the Empress of Wayland Hall," came back an instant concerted murmur of response.

"Contrary-minded?"

"No," piped up these two distinguished but extremely modest dancers.

"Two against eleven. Prepare to receive the prize." Ronny importantly opened the paper wrapper of the large package and took from it two sweet-grass square baskets of candied fruit. She presented them in turn with many bows and flourishes to the two elderly women.

"Who won the booby stunt?" she next demanded of the company.

Concerted opinion differed as to whether Jerry, or Kathie and Lillian were more eligible to the booby prize. Further inquiry and Jerry was eliminated in favor of Lillian and Kathie. The prizes turned out to be two small willow whistles such as the cow-boys at Manaña were adept at making.

"Next time whistle. Don't attempt to sing," was Ronny's succinct advice as she presented the would-be bass singers with the whistles.

"We can be noisy tonight and still be protected." Marjorie made gay declaration. She was realizing with the burst of light laughter which greeted Ronny's presentation of the booby prizes that the Travelers had been enjoying a most hilarious session. "Miss Remson is right here to know precisely how boisterous we are. Thank fortune, hardly anyone is back."

"I can't imagine why we haven't been notified of our noise by Miss Peyton," Jerry commented to Marjorie under cover of conversation.

As it happened Julia had become so greatly interested in her inspirational plan for a new sorority which was to tear down democracy at Hamilton and re-establish snobbery that she and Clara had forgotten to be annoyed at the sounds of mirth, which, in reality, could hardly be heard with her door closed.

"I took pains to find out today if any of the freshmen had studying to do this evening," the little manager said. "None had. I haven't considered Miss Peyton and Miss Carter in the matter. They have not yet spoken to me since they arrived. I am sure they have no studying to do this evening." Her tone grew dry at mention of the two discourteous juniors.

Immediately she went on to a change of subject. "Girls," she said in her brisk, pleasant fashion, "will you please make yourselves comfy, and listen to me? I am going to tell you something of the student whom I hope will take ."

"At last." Marjorie breathed a purposely audible sigh. "I think you have been very mysterious about her, Empress of Wayland Hall."

A buzzing murmur rose from the others as they took seats around the make-shift throne or comfortably established themselves upon cushions on the floor.

Leslie Cairns showed considerable embarrassment when Miss Susanna imperiously waved her into the middle seat of the throne. She had laughed unrestrainedly at the fun that evening, but she had said very little. She was hardly beginning to get over the strangeness of being a member of the very sorority she had once scorned.

"This girl," Miss Remson said, "is a young woman for whom I have a growing regard. She wrote me in the summer and I was deeply impressed by her letter. She did not then expect to enter Hamilton nor did I have in view for her. As it happened no one applied for . There was a difference in price between it and the other rooms I had vacant which no one who applied seemed to wish to pay.

"As soon as I knew that she was coming to Hamilton I reserved for her, though by that time I had several applications for it. I am waiting now to welcome her to Wayland Hall." Miss Remson made an odd little pause.

"We shall all be ready to do the same." Leila spoke in a peculiarly significant tone; as though she was understanding something which the others did not. Her bright blue eyes were fastened squarely upon Marjorie. They seemed to be trying to communicate a message to her.

In a sudden illuminating flash Marjorie understood the import of Miss Remson's remarks concerning the mysterious student who was to have Room .

"Oh, Miss Remson!" she breathed, her face breaking into a radiance of sunshine. Involuntarily her eyes strayed from Leila to Leslie. The latter was paying polite attention to Miss Remson though Marjorie divined instantly that Leslie had not comprehended a special meaning in the manager's speech.

"Will you come to the Hall, Leslie?" The little manager had turned now to Leslie, her thin pleasant face brimming with kindliness. "I should like you to have . I have been saving it for you since Marjorie told me you were to come back to Hamilton for your senior year."

"Why—I—" Leslie stammered. "Oh, I never thought of such a thing!" she exclaimed with bewildered gratitude. "It's wonderful in you to wish me to come back after the way I treated you. I'd love to, but I can't accept. It wouldn't be right." Tears crowded to her eyes. She clenched her hands and made a desperate effort at self-control.

"Now, now, now!" Up went one of Miss Remson's hands, arrestingly. "Never mind anything but the present, child. I wish you to have . That settles the matter. I must tell the girls a little more about your letter. Leslie wrote me last June, children, such a splendid letter."

"Hurrah, hurrah!" Vera had raised a subdued cheer. "Hurrah for our new Traveler in ." She started the hurrahing with the kindly object of giving Leslie an opportunity to control a threatened burst of tears. The others took up the cheering with moderated vigor.

"Please don't credit me with anything splendid, Miss Remson." Leslie forced tremulousness from her enunciation. "You girls understand me when I say that I couldn't have done differently, and feel right." She made a slight gesture of appeal toward the circle of faces approvingly turned upon her. "I might have known Miss Remson would tell you in the nicest way toward me. I meant to tell you all myself someday." She bent a half rueful glance of affection upon the little woman beside her.

"Ah, but you have not told us something else which we think you should." Leila had risen from the cushion on which she had been sitting. She came up to Leslie, hand extended. "Will you not accept the hand of fellowship and say: 'Thank you kindly, Irish Leila, it is myself that will be moving my trunks to Wayland Hall and be settling down in .'"

Leila's inimitable touch of brogue was irresistible to Leslie. She began to laugh. The two who had once been implacable enemies gripped hands with a friendly strength and fervor. It was a silent acknowledgment that, for them, there could be nothing in future less than devoted friendship. The deep-rooted disapproval of Leslie which Leila had not been able to conquer until within that very hour vanished never to return.

It was the signal for the others to press about Leslie, shaking her hand, each one adding some pleasant plea for her return to the Hall. Marjorie was last of the group to clasp hands with Leslie. She merely said, as she regarded the other girl with a bright, winsome smile: "Won't you please take , Leslie?"

"Yes." Leslie's tone was steady now. "How can I do otherwise? Not only because all of you wish me to do it. It's best for me, though it may be the hard way for a while. You understand what I mean."

"Yes. We all understand. We know what you wish most. You can make a stronger fight for it at the Hall than if you were to live off the campus. We'll all stand by you." Marjorie had taken Leslie's other hand. The two girls faced each other, staunch comradeship in the pose.

"I'll stand by myself." Leslie's characteristic independent spirit, obscured by emotion, flashed forth. "Not that I shan't like to remember that I've true pals ready to fight for me. But it's this way. Once I did a great deal of lawless damage on the campus. Now it's up to me to repair it, and stand all criticisms while I'm at the repairing job."

CHAPTER XVI.

PLANNING MISCHIEF

The appearance of Leslie Cairns the next week at Wayland Hall, followed by her trunk, temporarily drove Julia Peyton's club ambitions far afield. To discover that Leslie, to whom Julia liked to refer in shocked tones to others as "that terrible Miss Cairns," was to become a resident once more of Wayland Hall filled her with spiteful amazement and speculation.

"How do you suppose she ever got in here?" was the question she most frequently addressed to Clara Carter during the first two days following Leslie's return to the Hall. Neither she nor Clara had been able to glean any information in the matter from other students at the Hall. Wayland Hall was filling up rapidly. The upper classmen were busy arranging their programs and looking up their friends. The entering freshmen at the Hall were busy either with entrance examinations or unpacking and straightening their belongings.

To add to Julia's disgruntlement, Doris Monroe had been back at the Hall almost a week, yet not once had she noticed either Julia or Clara except by the distant courtesy of a bow or salutation whenever she chanced to encounter her two treacherous classmates.

Doris was far too greatly delighted with the way matters had shaped themselves for Leslie to think much of anything else. Of all the girls Leslie had known in her lawless days Doris had been the only one who had liked her for herself. From the day of Leslie's reconciliation with her father Doris and Leslie had continued their growing friendship on an even better basis than before. At last, each of the two girls knew the joy of claiming a real "pal."

Muriel had generously offered to release Doris from rooming with her, thus leaving her free to room in with Leslie. Not only did Doris refuse to take advantage of the offer, Leslie herself would not hear to it. "Stay where you are," she had laughingly ordered Doris. "I'll hang around with both of you." Secretly she courted the prospect of Muriel's enlivening company as a third in the chumship. More than once in the old days she had reluctantly admired "Harding's nerve."

When, in the course of a week, Julia learned that Leslie Cairns had re-entered Hamilton College as a member of the senior class her surprise at the news was soon superceded by a resentful desire to oust Leslie from Wayland Hall. Her jealous, vengeful disposition was an inheritance from her father, who bore the title of "Wolf Peyton" among Wall Street brokers where his offices were situated. Added to this grave flaw of character was her paramount will to gossip which had developed in her as a result of being the youngest child among three grown-up married sisters who were prone to gossip freely in her presence about friends and acquaintances.

For two weeks succeeding Leslie's advent at Wayland Hall, Julia racked her brain for a plan of malicious procedure which she might turn against Leslie. She consulted long and darkly with Clara Carter, whose ideas were not more feasible than her own.

"There's only one way to force Miss Remson to take action against Miss Cairns," she declared moodily to Clara one evening after dinner as the two sat down opposite each other at their study table.

"What's that?" Clara closed the Horace she had just opened and fixed expectant eyes upon Julia.

"Start a petition against having Miss Cairns in the house and then get the majority of students here to sign it. There's only one trouble. We need something specially definite to charge her with."

"Well, what about the Rustic Romp?" Clara instantly suggested.

"That doesn't amount to much." Julia shrugged scornfully. "Besides Miss Dean and Doris would fight for her if I started that story again. I don't care to have them interfering in this business. I'll have to be careful. I shall expect you to nominate me for president of our new club. I'll nominate you in return for vice-president. Caroline Phelps has promised to propose my name for class president. I'm letting her use my new car, you know. She ought to do something for me. However, that's not to the point about Miss Cairns. What I'd like to find out is just why she was expelled from Hamilton College."

"I thought you *knew*!" Clara opened innocent eyes. Here was an opportunity to nettle Julia. She seized it with avidity. "Why, it was for hazing. How strange that you——"

"You may think you are telling me something, but you are not." Julia grew emphatically rude. "I knew before ever you knew that it was for hazing. They say she and a crowd of girls, called the Sans Soucians Club, hazed Miss Dean. Did you know that?" she inquired, loftily incredulous.

"Of course I knew it. You told me that yourself, long ago."

"Oh." Julia showed a slightly crestfallen air. "It doesn't interest me," she continued after a moment. "I've heard that she would have been expelled long before that hazing affair if it hadn't been for her father's millions. What are some of the other things she did that might warrant expulsion here?

That's what I should like to know. It's what I'm going to find out. She made trouble between Doris and me. Doris only speaks to me when she can't avoid speaking. I'll never forgive Leslie Cairns for that." Julia's voice rose angrily.

"Sh-h-h. You are talking loudly." Clara held up a warning hand. "Someone passing through the hall might hear you."

Julia frowned, but discreetly lowered her voice. "If I can learn just one very dishonorable thing she did before she was expelled I can start the petition and carry it out. Most of the girls here are juniors, and will be on our side. You see last year Doris and Augusta Forbes were at swords' points at class election. Doris made a great mistake when she buried the hatchet after class election and was nice to Miss Forbes. The girls who rooted for her, and against Miss Forbes, are not going to forget in a hurry the way Doris went back on them. Now she is crazy about Miss Harper and Miss Dean and that provoking Miss Harding. *She* always looks as though she'd like to laugh in my face every time I happen to meet her on the campus, or in the house."

"I can't endure her." Clara was willing to agree with Julia regarding Muriel. More than once she had vaguely detected a furtive, laughing gleam in Muriel's velvety brown eyes when they had chanced to meet. "I'd love to be vice-president of our club. I'd not care to be president. You would make a better president than I—probably." She could not resist delivering this one tiny thrust.

"Naturally. I have more initiative than you." Julia retorted complacently. "I am more competent to manage a club than you would be. But you generally work very nicely with me," she allowed with condescension.

"I always try to, unless you are too provoking," Clara flung back. "How many girls at the Hall do you believe we can count upon already? I'll write down their names in the back of my note book." She was determined to show herself as extremely useful to Julia's scheme.

"Very well." Julia raised dignified brows. "First put down the name of Miss Ferguson and Miss Waters, those two freshies in . They are dandy girls. I'm rather glad now that I didn't make a fuss about the noise in that night before college opened. Miss Ferguson has told me since I met her that she heard it but was too good a sport to make a fuss. She said she detested a fusser, a dig, a prig or a wet blanket. When she was at Davidson Prep she said she used to cut classes and stay out after ten-thirty. Once she and another girl went to a dinner dance in New York without permission." Julia forgot dignity and grew animated. "Davidson is only a few miles from New York. They had asked permission of the registrar and she had refused them. They went just the same, came back at noon the next day and not a soul except the girls in the next room to them knew they were away. Wasn't that cunning?"

"Rash, I should say. I imagine I might like Miss Waters better than Miss Ferguson. She's not so swanky and flapperish."

"Go ahead then, and be nice to her. It will help our cause along," Julia advised with simulated heartiness. She craftily avoided arguing with Clara. Her disagreement with Doris of the previous spring had taught her at least one virtue. She could accomplish more by craftiness than by belligerency. She was doggedly determined upon one point—the utter humiliation of Leslie Cairns.

As maliciously as Leslie Cairns had once planned to humiliate Marjorie Dean, just as strongly Julia Peyton was now arrayed against Leslie Cairns.

CHAPTER XVII.

THE ONLY WAY

The junior class election taught Julia Peyton one unflattering truth. She was far from popular enough to win a nomination to the class presidency. Augusta Forbes directed her efforts, heart and soul toward the nomination of Doris Monroe. Doris as zealously rooted for Calista Wilmot, who had come to be greatly liked among the Hamilton students. Calista won the nomination by a majority of five votes and was subsequently elected president.

Notwithstanding the fact that Julia Peyton had not "a look in" at the presidency she was not without sympathetic support so far as a number of the juniors at Wayland Hall were concerned. These had been the sophs of the previous year of whom Leila Harper had signally disapproved. Then she had rated the Hall as a house divided against itself. With the opening again of the college she had not changed her opinion.

Counting Leslie Cairns she could number only fourteen staunch democrats at the Hall. There were now eight freshmen at the Hall whose politics were yet unannounced. Of the twenty-three other residents there was but one on whom she could rely as a neutral. This was Miss Duncan, a tall girl with a ministerial air who had succeeded in passing the set of "Brooke Hamilton Perfect Examination Papers" and had been awarded the special room at Wayland Hall set aside for this purpose. It had been vacant since Katherine Langly had attained that honor.

Hardly had the stir attending the junior election died away when Julia Peyton began agitating the subject of the select social sorority which she had been impatiently waiting to organize. She and Clara had privately decided that it should be called the "Orchid" Club—the name typifying, in her opinion, the select and exclusive.

Mildred Ferguson, the freshman in of whom Julia had glowingly spoken to Clara, had hailed the idea of the club with flattering enthusiasm. She was a small, slim girl with a pair of laughing blue eyes, a bright brown bob and a bold boyish face. She drove her own car, wore clothes of distinctive smartness and regarded everything in the way of luxury as having been produced for her benefit. She had had everything she fancied from babyhood. In consequence she never paused to consider anyone except herself. She was not interested in college except as a necessary bridge which had to be crossed into Society.

She soon found the poise of the post graduates at Wayland Hall not to her taste. The Bertram girls bored her, and she stood in secret awe of Doris Monroe and Leslie Cairns. Miss Duncan she dubbed the Eternal Dig. She found the more artificial standards of Julia Peyton, Clara Carter and their junior supporters more to her liking. She enjoyed having a "stand-in" with the juniors at the Hall and professed animated interest in the organizing of the Orchid Club. At heart she was so thoroughly snobbish as to agree with Julia's sentiments in regard to it.

Due to one delay or another, it was the early part of November before the Orchid Club, consisting of twenty-six members, held its first meeting in the living room of the Hall, Julia having haughtily requested the use of it from Miss Remson beforehand. To her deep satisfaction Julia was elected president of the club. Mildred Ferguson, however, won the vice-presidency, and with it Clara Carter's undying resentment.

There were no other offices to be filled. The Orchid Club was to be of a purely social nature, with no need of a secretary or treasurer. There was to be a dinner or luncheon twice each week at the expense of one or another of the club members, and a monthly meeting in the living room of the Hall.

"The Screech Owl has gone into local politics and is now a president," Muriel breezily informed Leslie Cairns and Doris Monroe as she entered Doris's and her room late one November afternoon to find the two deep in a discussion of psycho-analysis.

Leslie had taken up psychology and political science, the two subjects she had had on her senior program at the time of her expulsion from Hamilton. Thus far, since her return to Hamilton, she had wondered at the lack of unpleasant stir which had marked her reappearance on the campus as a student. It seemed that she might, after all, be fated to escape the harsh criticism which she felt would be justly her due. She had been agreeably disappointed in that Julia Peyton had not, to her knowledge, brought up against her as a matter of gossip the eventful night of the Rustic Romp.

"Julia Peyton a president?" Doris Monroe turned her blue-green eyes amusedly upon Muriel. "Of what, may I ask?"

"Of the Orchid Club. Isn't that a select name. It suggests luxury, doesn't it? Something like the Sans—I beg your pardon, Leslie." Muriel checked herself, looking comically contrite. "I never think of you now as a San," she went on in further apology.

"Don't mind me," Leslie waved off the apology. "You are exactly right in what you just said," she continued half grimly. "I have been keeping a wary eye upon Miss Peyton and Miss Carter since I came to the Hall. I fully expected they might start trouble for me. I am amazed to think they haven't.

Leila is right, too, in saying the Hall is a house divided against itself. It's not our side of it, though, that has put down a dividing line. By 'our side' I mean the Travelers, the Bertram girls and Doris. This Miss Peyton isn't the sort of menace to the Hall that I used to be." She smiled her slow smile. "She is like Lillian Walbert."

"Right-o," Muriel agreed with emphasis. "I'd forgotten all about her. Julia Peyton is more aggressive, though. Miss Walbert's favorite amusement was gossiping, just the same. Only she thought it was automobiling."

Muriel broke into a merry little run of laughter, an accompaniment to her mischievous statement regarding Lillian Walbert as a motorist.

"She was the worst flivver at driving a car that I ever recall having seen," Leslie said, her black eyes twinkling reminiscently. She was not likely to forget the many ridiculous situations in which Lillian figured at various times and points on Hamilton Highway as a result of her fatuous belief in herself as a driver.

"A gossip is never anything either clever, or useful," Doris Monroe observed with disdainful wisdom. "Julia Peyton is really quite stupid. She isn't consistent, even in her villainy. She never sticks to one story. This isn't intended as back-biting. I told her as much last spring. It is too bad she happened to be the one you tripped up with your umbrella, Leslie, at the Romp last spring. But I wouldn't let it worry me. Julia Peyton always over-reaches herself. If I should chance to hear any spiteful remarks from her of you—" Doris paused, smiling with dangerous sweetness.

"Goldie to the rescue. Thank you, good pal." Leslie flashed her a grateful glance. "I can fight my own fights. I'm not exactly crazy to get into the limelight here at the Hall, on my father's account. Still, I am not an ex-student who came back a doormat," she declared with dry significance.

She rose, smiled her slow smile at her companions and walked to the door. "See you later," she nodded. She opened the door and was gone.

"Oh, goodness." Muriel collapsed into a chair, self-vexation plainly evident on her pretty features. "I shouldn't have made that slip about the Sans. I am afraid I've hurt Leslie's feelings."

"No, you haven't." Doris shook a positive head. "I know Leslie better than you. She's worried about something; probably about Miss Remson. She is afraid, that, if Miss Peyton should begin gossiping about her, Miss Remson might be blamed for admitting her again to the Hall to board. That's why I just said to her that I'd fight for her."

"So will Miss Remson. She can fight her own battles, and Leslie's too," was Muriel's quick assurance.

In Room Leslie was at that moment dejectedly considering the very contingency Doris had mentioned to Muriel. Out of her long leadership of the Sans Soucians she had derived at least one benefit. She had learned to read character with surprising accuracy. A few days residence at Wayland Hall had put her in possession of the knowledge that Mildred Ferguson, rather than Julia Peyton, was the real promoter of the Orchid Club. Leslie had taken reflective stock of the self-assured smartly-attired freshman. Julia would be the club president in name only. Mildred would be the real power behind the throne. Mildred reminded her of Lola Elster, an ingrate whom she had boosted to campus popularity in the old days. Lola had had one commendable trait, however. She had ever tended strictly to her own affairs. Nor could any one persuade her to join any kind of campus conspiracy. She had "played safe" invariably to a disloyal degree. Mildred resembled her only in point of selfishness.

Leslie shrewdly rated Mildred as quarrel-seeking and gossiping, provided she might gain by adopting such a course. She was more formidable than Julia because she had a deceiving, attractive air of good-fellowship which she kept well over her hard, self-seeking nature.

What Leslie longed now to do was to make friendly overtures to Mildred before she should succeed in egging shallow, spiteful Julia Peyton on to "stir up a big fuss at the Hall." Leslie was satirically confident that she could, if she should try, quickly and effectually grow chummy with Mildred because of Peter Cairns' millions. She could soon influence Mildred to desert Julia's banner and enlist under hers. Mildred had already exhibited calculating signs of friendliness toward her.

Leslie somberly considered the idea from all sides, and shook a stern head. That was the easy way; the way made possible by money. It was the way she had always taken in the past. It had invariably brought her chagrin and failure. Now the rocky road of democracy must be her choice. Already she foresaw a condition of snobbery sprouting at the Hall which was similar to the one which Marjorie Dean had once fought to uproot.

"You are in for trouble, Cairns II," she said aloud. "You can't go placidly along about what you think is your business. Your business is to stand up for democracy—the way Marjorie Dean has always stood up for it. This Orchid crowd is going to give an imitation of the Sans at the Hall. I can see that. They need a change of policy. I'll have to try to supply it—in the right way." She laughed mirthlessly. "The right way" promised to be a rocky road indeed.

CHAPTER XVIII.

THE GREAT AND ONLY BIRTHDAY GIFT

Thanksgiving that year proved memorable enough to the Sanford girls. They had cheerfully decided against going home for the holidays and devoting themselves to the entertainment of the dormitory girls. Pending the completion of the dormitory the Hamilton College Bulletin had already announced the glad tidings of its advantages. As a result twice as many young women had applied for admission to the college that year and had arrived at Hamilton campus to be numbered with the colony of off-campus students who were living in the town of Hamilton at dormitory rates until the Brooke Hamilton Dormitory should be ready for occupancy.

On the day before Thanksgiving the Sanford girls had been ordered by Miss Susanna Hamilton to be ready to go to the station with her when she should stop for them at the western gates of the campus in her car at precisely one o'clock in the afternoon.

They had obeyed her mandate and gone with her to the station there to behold Mr. and Mrs. Dean, Mr. and Mrs. Macy, and Hal, Mr. and Mrs. Harding, Mrs. Warner, and the two Misses Archer, Ronny's aunts, step beaming off the one-five train from the north. Leila, Vera, Kathie, Doris Monroe, Robin, Phil and Barbara and Leslie Cairns had also been invited to the largest house party that Hamilton Arms had ever seen invade its stately doors. Leslie's joy had soared to dizzy heights when the first person she had spied at the Arms was her father, standing bare-headed on the veranda, waiting for her.

Following Thanksgiving and the delightful season of merry-making at the Arms the Travelers found December flying and Christmas approaching with astonishing rapidity. This time the Sanford girls went to Sanford for Christmas, taking Miss Susanna and their six Traveler chums with them. Leslie and Doris spent Christmas in New York with Peter Cairns, a vastly merrier and happier Christmas than they had spent in the metropolis the previous year.

There had been no need for any of the original chapter of Travelers to remain on the campus, there to oversee the making of a merry Christmas for the dormitory students. The senior "dorms" had become thoroughly competent in the matter of providing Christmas amusement for the off-campus dormitory colony. During the month of December, Leila, Kathie, Robin and Phillys Moore had applied themselves zealously to the pleasant task of arranging a couple of one-act plays and various other interesting entertainments. They had, as a consequence, embarked on their trip to Sanford with a pleasant sense of work well done.

Leslie Cairns, of all the Travelers, had perhaps felt most sincerely the true spirit of Christmas. Never before in her life had she quite understood the meaning of "Peace on earth, good will toward men." Even as a child she had not enjoyed the ineffably beautiful comradeship that now existed between herself and her father. He in turn was fondly proud of her fine spirit of resolution. She confided to him her determination to try to do her part toward keeping up the spirit of democracy which the original Travelers had fought so gallantly to establish and maintain.

"There's only one drawback to it all, Peter the Great," she had said to her father during one of their firelight confabs. "If this crowd of snobs at the Hall should start on me for anything I may feel it right to do, contrary to their ideas, it would be bound to reflect upon you. That is, if these girls should drag up that hazing business against me. You'd be criticized, maybe, for not bringing me up with a stern hand, and all that sort of talk. But I've struck a certain gait, Peter, and I'm going to keep it. Maybe I'm borrowing trouble. Maybe the blow I'm always dreading may never fall."

It was in such spirit that Leslie returned to the campus after the holidays. On the afternoon of her return to Wayland Hall she was notified by Leila that a hope chest party which the Travelers had planned as a surprise for Marjorie was to take place that night at Hamilton Arms. Since early in the fall the hope chest party had been in the offing.

During the previous summer each of Marjorie's Traveler chums had picked out a gift which was to go in a special carved rosewood chest which Miss Susanna had been hoarding for her favorite. Leila had brought Marjorie a wonderful package of fine Irish table linen. Vera had selected a frock of rose-pattern Irish lace. Ronny's gift was an amethyst necklace in an old Peruvian setting. Each of the others had searched faithfully to find a gift which she considered worthy of the girl who had long been their leader.

It had been left to Miss Susanna to name the date of the party. She had named the fifth of January as the date, though none of the Travelers knew why.

"It's a case of hustle off the train, flee for the campus, gobble one's dinner and be off again merry-making," Muriel declared animatedly as the hope chest partly stepped out into the starlight after dinner that evening and set buoyantly off across the campus for a jolly hike.

Jerry and Leila had been intrusted with the combined offerings of the surprise party and had preceded the others to the Arms in Leila's car. They had been instructed by their companions to park the car just inside the gates in the shadow where Miss Susanna had ordered George, the stable man, to be on hand to look after the car and its precious contents. According to a mysterious plan of Leila's, which she laughingly refused to divulge, the presents were to make an appearance considerably later in the evening.

After dinner at the Arms that evening Jonas had managed to disappear and Miss Susanna had innocently requested, "Go to the door, child. Will you please?" when the clang of the old-time knocker rang out resonantly.

Willingly constituting herself doorkeeper in Jonas's absence Marjorie opened the door and was immediately swept into the great reception hall on a buoyant tide of youthfully exhilarated chums.

"Why, whatever is the matter?" Miss Susanna appeared in the open door of the library trying hard to look shocked by the noise. Her small face was full of gleeful mischief over having thus taken Marjorie quite off her guard.

"Yes, whatever is the matter?" Marjorie made one of her open-armed rushes at the old lady. "You can see for yourself now. You dear Goldendede." She hugged Miss Susanna. "How did you know I needed a surprise party more than anything else?"

"Oh, this isn't your party," chuckled Miss Hamilton. "I only allowed you to be surprised. This is my party. Today," she tilted her head sideways at a bird-like angle, "is my birthday. Now don't smother—"

Her warning was lost in the jolly concerted shout that went up from the surprise guests. They surrounded her, hemmed her in; kissed her until her face was rosy. Jerry even threatened to administer a birthday whipping. It was the one thing which the girls had long been curious to find out. Miss Susanna had steadily refused to divulge her birth date even to Marjorie.

"And we haven't a single present for you," wailed Vera regretfully.

"So much the better. There's nothing I need except more love. I'm rich in that, by the Grace of God." Miss Susanna had emerged from the affectionate wooling she had received, radiantly smiling.

Then began one of the delightful evenings, which, instead of being few and far between, were now frequent occurrences in the contented life of the once pessimistic mistress of the Arms. As it neared nine o'clock Leila announced that she had a fine stirring song to sing and invited Robin to vacate the piano stool.

"Miss Susanna may have heard this gem. I am sure the rest of you have not," she declared with beaming smiles. "It is called 'Wait for the Wagon.' It is a deeply significant song." She turned to the piano and began a jerky little prelude which Phil said sounded exactly like the jolting of a wagon. Leila then lifted up her voice in a creaky old-fashioned tune which convulsed her listeners.

She sang two verses amid ripples of laughter. Nothing dismayed by the laughing derision accorded her vocal efforts she vigorously began a third. Then something happened. Down the hall outside came the approaching squeak of wheels. The laughter rose to a mild shout as Jonas appeared in the doorway, pulling after him a good-sized toy express wagon piled high with fancy-wrapped, be-ribboned bundles. Strangely enough each package was tied with pale violet satin ribbon. He trundled the wagon into the room and to where Marjorie sat, winsome and laughing, saying: "Miss Susanna says that she has the birthday, but you may have the presents."

"Oh! Why! I don't need any!" Marjorie exclaimed, looking abashed. "It's not my birthday."

"No, but you've a wedding day coming," Miss Susanna said, matter-of-fact and smiling, "and a hope chest, too. Go and bring it, Jonas. Open your hope gifts, child, and be glad your friends aren't stingy." In spite of her prosaic tone there was a tender gleam in her bright brown eyes.

She lost it immediately and began to laugh at Jonas who turned solemnly and trundled the wagon into the hall and out of sight. He came creaking back again soon with the beautiful rosewood chest.

Surrounded by a love knot of friends, Marjorie opened package after package, smiling at first, but tenderly tearful toward the last. She was especially touched by Jonas's gift to her of a gorgeous Chinese vase which Brooke Hamilton had given him and which had been one of his few treasures. She also dropped two or three tears on an exquisite jade figure which Leslie Cairns had given her. She understood it to be a reminder of the momentous afternoon when she had worn the jade frock and they had gone together to President Matthews' office.

When she had opened, loved and exclaimed over the last gift, a hand-embroidered lunch cloth from Kathie, every stitch of which had been taken by her patient fingers, she turned from the library table, now gaily blossoming with her riches, and opened both arms in a gesture of endearment.

"I haven't any words dear enough to tell you in how much I love you, and thank you," she said. "I only know I do. It seems to me my life has been nothing but a succession of glorious surprises. I think I've been given so much more than my share of love and happiness."

A chorus of fond dissent greeted her earnestly humble words.

"Sh-h. That's only half of my speech." She held up a playfully admonishing finger. "The other half is about Miss Susanna. It's something I've been wishing to ask her a long time. Because she has loved me in the same way Captain and General have loved me I have the courage to ask this great favor. Captain and General know I am going to ask it. So does Hal. Please, Goldendede, dear Goldendede, may Hal and I be married at the Arms on Mr. Brooke's birthday?"

"*May you?*" Miss Susanna got up from her chair and came straight to Marjorie. On her small, keen face shone the light of a great devotion. "May you?" she repeated. "How could you know, child, that this was what I wished for most. I never dared mention it to you. It seemed so selfish in me. You've given me the great and only birthday present."

CHAPTER XIX.

LET WELL ENOUGH ALONE

"At last I've discovered what I've been dying to find out!" Julia Peyton burst into the room occupied by herself and Clara Carter, her black, moon-like eyes full of excitement.

"Have you?" Clara made an elaborate pretense of indifference. She kept her eyes fastened on the book before her on the study table. She was thoroughly peeved with Julia for having gone across the hall to see Mildred Ferguson at least an hour before.

Julia had returned to Hamilton on the previous afternoon. Clara had not returned, however, until that afternoon. She thought Julia might have shown more interest in seeing her. Instead, she had hurried to Mildred Ferguson's room directly after dinner on the plea of consulting with Mildred about the Orchid Club's next luncheon.

"Oh, drop your book, and listen to me." Julia sat down on the edge of her couch bed with an impatient bounce.

"Why should I? You haven't stopped to consider me?" Clara retorted, frost in her tones. "But it doesn't matter. Please say what you wish. I am interested in this story. I began it on the train and I'm anxious to finish it tonight. I shan't have time to-morrow."

"Oh, bother your old story!" Julia exclaimed. "You are simply peeved. The story I have to tell you is a good deal more interesting than the one you're reading. I have just heard the true story of Leslie Cairns. What do you think of that?" Julia was full of malicious elation.

"True story?" Clara returned interrogatively. She refused to let curiosity interfere with her miffed assumption of dignity.

"Yes, the true story of how she led the girls she chummed with into a hazing party and then tried to lay the whole thing to them so as to save herself from being expelled. That's the sort of person *she* is."

"I suppose Mildred Ferguson told you all this," Clara said coolly. "Where did she find out so much? How do you know what she says is true?"

"She found out about Miss Cairns from a cousin. The cousin was one of the girls who chummed with Miss Cairns, and who was with the hazing party. I believe every word of what she told me." Julia crested her head in displeased defiance of Clara.

"Mm-m." Clara unbent a trifle. "Who is her cousin? When did she hear about Miss Cairns? Off the campus, I believe. I've never found anyone on the campus who knew the rights of that hazing business. They say Miss Dean knows. She ought to, since she was the student those girls hazed. She'd never tell anyone a word about it, though."

"She may keep her information," shrugged Julia scornfully. "I know more about it now, perhaps, than she does. I mean, I know the Cairns side of it. You see Mildred's cousin is a very rich girl named Dulcie Vale. She is a society favorite, but she was a senior at Hamilton when it all happened."

"Then she must have been expelled from Hamilton, too." Clara put in half contemptuously. "All those San Soucians were expelled."

"She was not," Julia emphasized, frowning. "She left Hamilton before it happened because she knew that Leslie Cairns had betrayed the whole crowd of girls by being too confidential with another student named Miss Walbert, who was noted on the campus as a tale-bearer and gossip."

"I thought they were *all* expelled," Clara persisted obstinately.

"Miss Vale was *not*." Julia showed signs of becoming exasperated. "Please listen to me, Clara. This is very important for you to know. That is, if you care to do your part toward making Wayland Hall a house free from such derogatory influences as Miss Cairns is bound sooner or later to exert."

"That's one way of putting it." Clara laid aside her book. Her pale blue eyes shot sparks of resentment at Julia. "I happen to know you a little better than anyone else here knows you."

"Of course you do." Julia controlled her temper with an effort. She was more anxious to tell Clara what she had heard about Leslie than she was to squabble with Clara. "That's precisely why I am trying to give you my confidence," she explained, with pretended warmth.

"Hm-m. Go ahead, then." Somewhat mollified, Clara gave in. She had defeated her curiosity several times. Now she decided to gratify it.

"Mildred's mother is Dulcie Vale's aunt," Julia began with impressive alacrity. "The Vale family held a re-union in New York this year over New Year's. Dulcie's father is the president of the L., T. and M. Railroad, and is worth a lot of money. But not as much as Miss Cairns' father is worth. Dulcie and Mildred met at the re-union. They hadn't seen each other for almost four years. Mildred thought Dulcie was a Vassar graduate. She was surprised to hear that Dulcie had attended Hamilton. Dulcie was surprised to know that Mildred was a Hamilton freshman. She began asking Mildred all sorts of questions about the campus and Wayland Hall."

Julia paused to take breath, then continued with relish: "Mildred said Dulcie positively went up in the air when she heard that Leslie Cairns was back at Hamilton. Then she started in and told Mildred the whole story of the whole time she and Miss Cairns were at Hamilton together. Mildred said she couldn't begin to remember all Dulcie told her against Miss Cairns. For one thing Miss Cairns hired a coach to teach her team a lot of dishonest basket ball tricks. Then she tried to make the other girls on the team, who were all Sans, learn them. Dulcie was on the team. She absolutely refused to do a thing that was unfair in the game. That made Leslie Cairns angry with her. After that they were never friendly again, but Dulcie stood a good many things because she wanted to be loyal to the Sans.

"Then Miss Cairns ran Miss Langly down, speeding on Hamilton Pike. She tried to pretend it was another motorist who had done it. She had to own up to it, though. She had to go before Prexy, and was nearly expelled that time."

"How did they haze Miss Dean? Did Miss Vale say?" Clara was in hopes of hearing what she longed to discover.

"Oh, they dressed up in dominos and masks and walked Miss Dean around the campus two or three times. It was on Valentine's night. That's the junior masquerade night, you know. Then they were going to let her go, but Leslie Cairns said they shouldn't. She and three or four of the Sans took Miss Dean to an empty house and locked her in it. Dulcie and most of the others went straight back to the gym to the dance."

"Then they shouldn't have been expelled," Clara declared stolidly. "They should have been able to clear themselves."

"None of the Sans would have been expelled if Miss Cairns had been loyal to them. She told this Miss Walbert about it, and that Dulcie was to blame for the whole thing. Miss Walbert told every girl she knew on the campus. The story went on till the faculty got hold of it. Somehow it was reported to Prexy. Dulcie found out from his secretary, who was her friend, that Prexy was going to bring the Sans on the carpet for hazing. She went to Leslie and warned her to be on her guard. Leslie said she had been telling tales. She set the other Sans against Dulcie, and they treated her so outrageously she had a nervous collapse, and had to leave college. She wrote President Matthews a lovely letter before she left, saying how sorry she was to have to leave Hamilton. It must have impressed him greatly." Julia rolled her moon-like eyes. "He sent for Leslie Cairns soon afterward. Then she turned against her chums and the upshot was that they were all expelled. Only she didn't expect that she would be. Do you consider such a girl a good influence at the Hall? I don't." She replied to her own question with vindictive stress.

"But suppose this Dulcie Vale hadn't told the truth?" Clara did not like Mildred. She was therefore ready to doubt the integrity of Mildred's cousin.

"She's told it nearly enough so that we know what happened," Julia maintained in a slightly sullen tone. "Besides we aren't going to put everything I've just told you in the petition. We shall simply base the petition upon what we know."

"Hm-m." Clara vented her favorite satiric ejaculation. "You'll have to show the girls in the club, or else they will refuse to sign it. You can't simply state in it that Leslie Cairns is an undesirable person to have at the Hall. You'll have to substantiate your accusations."

"You must think we are infants. What makes you so snippy, Clara Carter? We have arranged for everything. The girls in the Orchid Club will sign the petition after Mildred goes before them at a special meeting. Dulcie Vale is going to send Mildred a tabulated account of Leslie Cairns' doings here. She will read it out to the club. Then I think they will be ready to sign the petition. After that—" Julia curled a confident lip. "The majority rules, you know. We are twenty-six against twenty. At least half a dozen of that twenty will not take sides. That makes it a matter of only fourteen against twenty-six."

"Miss Remson will fight against making Miss Cairns leave the Hall. She seems to like her. It seems queer to me that Miss Remson would take her back again, and be so sweet to her. And Miss Dean and her crowd! Miss Cairns is awfully chummy with them." Deep within Clara a stubborn doubt had risen as to the feasibility of Julia's vengeful scheme.

It had begun to form before Christmas as a result of Julia's crush on Mildred. Clara had sulked matters out alone. As a result she had freed herself to a certain extent from Julia's spiteful influence. And the beneficial result of frequent hours spent alone was a general pulling-up in her classes and a lack of impulse to gossip, since she had not Julia to gossip with. She was beginning to lean toward a more charitable state of mind though she had not yet discovered it.

"Miss Remson may fuss all she pleases about the petition. We shall appeal to Prexy and demand justice."

"How do you suppose Miss Cairns got back on the campus?" Clara laughed a trifle scornfully. "By Prexy's permission, of course. Of what use then to appeal to him? You'd best let well enough alone. You'll never win. I am saying it to you for your own good, Julia."

"Much obliged, I'm sure." Julia was now thoroughly incensed. "I don't in the least understand you, Clara. I do know this. We shall win. We are prepared to take it even above Prexy's head, and to the College Board. We shall have our parents take up the matter, if necessary. You were in sympathy with us at first. Now—" She sprang up from the couch and walked to the door, her black eyes smouldering with anger. "All I'll ask of you is not to repeat what I've just said. You must do as you think wise about signing the petition." She went out the door, closing it after her with a sharp little bang.

"Julia had best let well enough alone," Clara repeated aloud as she resumed her book. "She'll never win."

CHAPTER XX.

A BRAVE RESOLVE

"The Orchid Club is most certainly in an enthusiastic state," Vera Mason remarked tranquilly as she raised her eyes from a bit of difficult Greek prose and listened to the faint, concerted sounds of applause that ascended in waves from behind the closed doors of the living room.

"A regular gale of glee," Leila spoke with a faint touch of good-humored satire. "What is it that calls for such applause, I wonder?"

"We shall never know." Vera made a gesture of resigned futility. "Their worthy president has forgotten how much she objected to our demonstrations of joy in last year. They are making a great deal more noise than ever we made."

"They are welcome to make it. Shut up in the living room, they are at least out of mischief." Leila promptly forgot the demonstrative assemblage below stairs in the writing of a stirring scene in the "melodramer" she had long promised Robin and Marjorie she should one day write. She had named it "The Fatal Message," and it abounded in scenes, villains and thrilling situations to a ludicrous extent. The hero's name was Rupert and the heroine's Madelene. The greater part of the stage scenery belonging to Leila's theatrical paraphernalia divided the lovers throughout the play until they met in the palatial drawing room of Madelene's long-lost millionaire father in the last scene of the fifth act.

As usual Augusta Forbes had been selected for the heroic part of Rupert. Gentleman Gus had acquired great glory as a portrayer of male roles. Because the Hamilton girls loved to see her grace the stage in her golden beauty, Doris Monroe had been selected to play the part of Madelene. In ministerial-appearing Miss Duncan, Leila had also discovered a treasure. Miss Duncan had proved upon acquaintance to be as humorous and jolly as she seemed staid and severe. She had confessed a longing to swank about the stage in male attire and had covered herself with glory as Henry the Fifth in three scenes from the splendid play which had been given at a "Shakesperian Show" managed by Page and Dean.

"Shut up in the living room," however, the Orchid Club were hardly verifying Leila's light supposition. A week had passed since Julia Peyton had triumphantly boasted to Clara Carter that she had found the means she had been seeking to drive Leslie Cairns from Wayland Hall. All she and Mildred

Ferguson lacked toward starting the ball of injustice rolling was the promised tabulated list from Dulcie Vale.

Dulcie had not seen Leslie since the two girls had been students at Hamilton. She had known herself to be so thoroughly despised by Leslie and the other Sans for her treachery toward them that she had preferred to keep at a distance from them. She had once met and greeted Joan Myers and had received a snubbing which she never forgot. In her heart she had the same old envious dislike for Leslie as in the days on Hamilton campus when she had resented Leslie's undeniable sway over the Sans.

During the interval of more than two years which had elapsed since the downfall of the San Soucians at Hamilton College, Dulcie Vale had not improved either in wisdom or truth. She had the same lack of regard for the truth as ever. When she had discovered at the Vale's New Year's re-union that Mildred Ferguson was a student at Hamilton, and had also learned to her nettled amazement that Leslie Cairns had by some means or other managed to return to Hamilton, she immediately planned mischief. She was as ready to drag Leslie down into the dust of humiliation as ever.

It was with malicious pleasure that she set to work on the tabulated list of Leslie's misdeeds the day following the re-union. She spent the greater part of three days composing and arranging the list, then mailed it to Mildred with satisfaction. It had arrived in the afternoon mail of the previous day and the Orchid Club had been notified to a member to be on hand at eight o'clock in the living room of the Hall on the next evening.

Julia and Mildred had spent the entire evening previous to that of the meeting in drawing up the fateful petition. Due to Mildred's selfish ability to steer conveniently clear of snags, the petition was worded so cleverly as to carry the effect of a protest against deep injury reluctantly stated. It began:

"We, the undersigned do hereby make plea for a condition of affairs at Wayland Hall which shall be in entire harmony with the ideals and traditions of Hamilton College."

Followed in "the interests of truth and honor" a dignified protest against Leslie Cairns' presence at the Hall. The petition ended with the crafty assurance that three representatives from among the objectors were prepared to state in private conference with Miss Remson their objections to Leslie Cairns as a resident of Wayland Hall.

While Julia Peyton had a known grievance against Leslie, Mildred also had one, though it was less tangible. She had shrewdly estimated Leslie at sight as a person of some consequence. She had accordingly decided to cultivate Leslie's acquaintance. She had met with a peculiar kind of defeat. She had all of a sudden understood that Leslie understood her. She sensed as clearly as though it had been said to her that Leslie had quickly plumbed her soul and discovered her ignoble motive for making friendly advances. On this very account she felt aggressive toward Leslie, as is the way with persons of small nature. She was quite content with Julia's determination to shame Leslie.

Mildred had chosen to read out Dulcie Vale's list to the members of the club. This to Julia's only half concealed disappointment. She had allotted the reading of the petition to Julia, who had accepted the minor honor somewhat distantly. The reading of the petition evoked far more applause than did Dulcie's letter, which was gratifying to Julia. She took the credit for its composition though Mildred had dictated its policy.

As a matter of fact the members of the Orchid Club were rather horrified at the list of offenses Dulcie had tabulated against Leslie. The psychological effect produced upon the company by the reading of the list was decidedly unpleasant. They were a thoughtless, pleasure-loving group of girls with undoubted snobbish tendencies. They were not in any sense embued with the spirit of lawlessness which had brought the Sans to grief. Nevertheless the list served its purpose to the extent that the majority of the club were in instant favor of presenting the petition to Miss Remson.

There were a few faint-hearted objections to the proposal from four or five girls who presented the arguments that Miss Cairns had powerful friends at the Hall in the post graduates, that Miss Remson would fight for Leslie and that Prexy might be a good friend of Miss Cairns' father. These arguments were energetically swept aside by Julia and Mildred, who made mysterious promises to take the matter "higher" with the surety of receiving justice from the College Board should both Miss Remson and Prexy prove partial.

"In the face of all Miss Cairns has done against the traditions and rules of Hamilton it would be *nothing but partiality* for President Matthews to refuse to honor our petition." Julia had risen to argue as eloquently against Leslie as a district attorney might have against a murderer. "If he should do this then we must come out boldly and accuse him of partiality. We shall have our parents write letters of protest to him, and to the Board."

While her hearers were not altogether satisfied with her arguments neither were they pleased to have Leslie at the Hall. They had the innate tendency of well-bred girls toward the keeping of honorable company which in other circumstances might have been commendable.

It was Mildred, however, who put the final touch to Julia's harangue. "Oh, what is the use of being afraid to sign that petition?" she demanded, her blue eyes laughing scorn at her clubmates. It was the one thing needed to decide them against Leslie. "What harm can it do you? Haven't you a right to the courage of your convictions? You can't be executed, you know, for signing.

Incidentally we may win. Think it over, then start at the left and come up to the table and sign. But take your chairs again. We have other business to transact before the close of the meeting."

Leslie, coming in later from a little expedition of her own, encountered the chattering throng of girls as it poured into the hall from the living room. In crossing the hall to the stairs she was curiously aware of a stir among the chatterers which she could not but lay to her appearance among them. She bade the students nearest to her a reserved good evening and hurried on up the stairs feeling vexed with herself for the odd premonition which had flashed through her mind of the approach of something disagreeable. She shook off the feeling, impatiently attributing it to the constant expectation of being harshly criticised which she unwillingly harbored.

Since the beginning of her senior year Leslie had quietly interested herself in the poor of the town of Hamilton. Her program of only two subjects gave her ample time to look about her. She had more money than she could possibly spend. She no longer cared about spending it like water for fancied costly luxuries. Her idea of charity consisted in buying a car full of groceries and necessities, then driving around among the needy families in the lower part of the town and making them happy. She never stopped to inquire whether they were worthy. She simply gave as her sympathies directed. Already she had planned, that, when she and Peter the Great should come to live at Carden Hedge, she would ask him to establish some sort of industry in South Hamilton which should provide work for the poor there at a living wage.

The day following the meeting Leslie came to a grim conclusion that "something must be stirring" against her among her housemates. It was the first time since her advent at the Hall that she had noticed anything so general as the peculiarly disapproving aloofness which showed itself among the tables full of girls as she went into the dining room to breakfast. By night she had become convinced of her suspicion. She set her jaws and brought an intrepid spirit to bear upon the threatening situation. Whatever it might be she would not go whining with it to Miss Remson. She would not run out to meet calamity, either. But, if calamity came, she would walk bravely out to meet it, alone.

CHAPTER XXI.

A SURPRISE FOR THE ORCHID CLUB

"Please, Miss Leslie, Miss Remson says will you come to her room and bring Miss Monroe with you? She'd like to see you right away." Annie beamed her whole-hearted regard upon Leslie, to whom she was indebted for various pleasant gratuities.

"I'll be with her in ten minutes. Miss Monroe has gone out to mail a letter. She'll be back directly." Leslie closed the door upon Annie's retreating back with slow reflectiveness. "I wonder," she murmured: "I wonder."

"Miss Remson just sent Annie for us," she said to Doris as the latter entered, her perfect face in charming relief against the dark bear's fur collar of her coat. Her head was bare and her hair was massed gold in the lamplight.

"For us?" Doris lifted her dark brows. "Why?"

"Don't know. I think I'm due to hear something unpleasant," Leslie returned with frowning conviction. "I saw it coming this morning."

"Saw what coming?" Doris looked concerned. "I mean, what did you see?"

Leslie explained as well as she could. "I can't kick, you know. Here it is, January, and I've had smooth sailing. But I'm going to hit the rocks, I guess. The question is: Who supplied the rocks, and how big are they?" Leslie finished with mocking humor.

"If you really are correct in your suspicion, Leslie, you can blame Julia Peyton for the whole thing," Doris spoke with anxious warmth. "She supplied the rocks, if there are any. But she is so untruthful, no one will take her word long for anything. She has probably woven a weird tale about the Rustic Romp. I'll soon put a stop to it if I can find out what she has said."

"It may not be that at all." Leslie shook her head. "It's more apt to be something I did when I was on the campus before. I did so many things I shouldn't have done. She may have happened to unearth one of them. Well," unconsciously Leslie squared her shoulders, "let's go and see."

"Come in, girls." To their surprise Doris and Leslie found Miss Remson standing in the door of her upstairs sitting room, evidently on watch for them. She beckoned the girls into the room and closed the door quickly.

"There," she declared, "I am as well pleased to have no one see you. I am so angry. Gr—r—r!" The little woman accompanied the growl with a violent shake of the head. "I know you'd prefer me to be direct, Leslie. Read this." She handed Leslie a folded paper. "Then we'll talk."

Leslie unfolded the sheet, scanned it eagerly, then passed it on to Doris with a bitter little laugh. "Here's the rock," she said. "It's a big one."

"Outrageous!" Doris cried out indignantly, letting the fateful petition flutter to the floor.

Leslie picked it up and re-read it. "No one is to blame but myself," she asserted doughtily. "I'll not have you annoyed, Miss Remson, by anything I'm responsible for. I'll leave the Hall tomorrow and go back to the Hamilton House. At least I've Prexy's permission to finish my course here."

"You'll *not* leave the Hall, Leslie. Such a contemptible thing for a crowd of girls to do," Miss Remson's eyes showed an angry sparkle.

"Not half so bad as the things I——"

"Now, now, Leslie. This is the present, you know." Miss Remson said soothingly. "That petition is only the beginning. Read this. But, first, glance at the signature." She tendered Leslie a thicker fold of paper.

"Dulcie Vale!" Leslie's voice rose in astonishment as she scanned the well-remembered signature: "Dulciana Maud Vale." "Now I begin to understand what it's all about. Please, pardon me, both of you, while I give Dulcie's latest outbreak the once-over. 'The Leslie Cairns' List,'" she read out. "That's exactly like Dulcie Vale, the little stupid."

Miss Remson waited silently for Leslie to read the several sheets of typed paper. At last she glanced up with a laugh of satirical amusement. "Dulcie must have hired a stenographer to type this. She never typed it herself," was her characteristically unexpected comment. "Here is a full account of the crimes of Cairns, Doris. Only Dulcie has tied the truth up in an awful snarl. Read about me in this monograph. If you are still my friend after you read it, you deserve a friendship medal."

"That petition was handed to me last night after the meeting in the living room," Miss Remson said. "I read it, and went to Miss Peyton before the ten-thirty bell rang. Her name heads the list, you see. I suspected her as being at the bottom of the trouble. I told her very sternly that I should expect to meet her committee of three next day at noon in my office. Today at noon Miss Ferguson came to my office with a great pretence of dignity. She brought with her this outrageous piece of spite work," she indicated the list Doris was perusing, her beautiful face utterly impassive.

"She said she would prefer me to read the list she handed me, then she, Miss Peyton and Miss Waters would meet me in conference. At first I thought of handing the list and petition back to her with a lecture. Instead, I accepted the list and said that I would take up the matter with them in three days. As yet I had nothing to say. They went away. There was nothing else for them to do." Miss Remson's lips tightened.

"Once upon a time, Leslie," she continued, "Ronny Lynne and I held a meeting in the living room. You remember why."

"Yes, I remember." Leslie flushed. "I wish I had been wise enough to profit by the experience of that evening."

Miss Remson referred to the eventful evening during Leslie's sophomore year at Hamilton when she had called a meeting in the living room of Wayland Hall in order to see justice done to Marjorie Dean. Leslie had then been the prime mover in an unworthy attempt to traduce Marjorie which had ended in deserved defeat for Leslie.

"Forgive me for mentioning it." The little manager flashed Leslie a smile of stanch friendship. "History may repeat itself. I wish you would leave this matter entirely to me, Leslie. Think nothing further of it. Don't consider leaving the Hall. This report of you compiled by Dulcie Vale is grossly untrue."

"It is, of course, garbled. It's an entirely different story of the hazing than the one she wrote in the letter to President Matthews. That was our finish at Hamilton. Dulcie ought to do well writing fiction." In the midst of her dejection Leslie could not refrain from this humorous thrust at Dulcie.

"It's too bad, Leslie." Doris looked up from the papers in her hand, her tone one of affection. "You are doing your best to make up for what you once did that wasn't honorable. We all make plenty of mistakes. Only it takes a brave person to go back and try to retrieve them. I'll stand by you. So will the Travelers." She came over to where Leslie sat, elbow on chair, chin in hand, her dark face immobile as an Indian's. She put a reassuring arm across Leslie's shoulders.

"You are a good pal, Goldie." Leslie raised her head from her hand in an upward appreciative glance. "I've always said that, even when we squabbled."

"I shall continue to be a good pal," Doris assured, smiling. Secretly she intended to find a means, if she could, to make the signers of the petition feel ashamed and foolish.

When the two friends left Miss Remson's sitting room a few moments later Doris went to her own room instead of stopping in Leslie's. There she found Muriel industriously writing to her fiancé, Harry Lenox.

"Tell me about a meeting that once took place in the living room downstairs because of something Leslie said about Marjorie," she began abruptly.

"Um-m. Wait a minute until I have wound up my weekly love letter to my intended," giggled Muriel. "That's what Annie calls the plumber she is going to marry. My intended!" Muriel repeated the phrase admiringly. "Isn't that sweet?"

"How romantic you are!" Doris duplicated the giggle.

"Ain't I jist?" Muriel came back buoyantly. "You ought to read my letters to Harry. They are almost business-like enough to be signed 'Yours very truly.' Would you like me to read you this one?"

"Mercy, no. I should not care to hear it." Doris said with amused stress.

"And I shouldn't care to read it to you," Muriel replied with great affability.

"Nor to tell me about that meeting, either," reminded Doris slyly.

"Oh, yes, the meeting." Muriel appeared to remember vaguely Doris's question. "Why don't you ask—. No, you wouldn't care to do that." Muriel stopped, surveying Doris quizzically.

"You mean ask either Leslie or Marjorie," Doris said quickly. "Not if I can help it."

"What has happened?" Muriel continued to eye Doris shrewdly.

"That's what I should like to tell you."

"Don't be afraid to confide in me," Muriel assured flippantly. Sobering her merry features, she added: "I'll tell you about the meeting." She snapped her fountain pen shut, leaned back in her chair and recounted a trifle sketchily the happenings of the eventful meeting in the living room in which Marjorie had figured so prominently.

"Poor Leslie." Doris shook her head pityingly after Muriel had finished the little story. "What a lot of trouble she has made for herself in the past. I'm so glad everything is different with her now. I'm glad I found myself in time. We girls who've been left without our mothers when we are children to grow up in the care of servants are bound to be selfish, even unprincipled. What ought I to do, Muriel? You are so clever at suggestion. I have an idea that the way to deal with these girls is to show them themselves from the standpoint of foolishness. Such attempts from a group of students at injuring another student are so terribly underbred, I think."

A sudden mischievous smile overspread Muriel's face. "I know a good way to do," she said. She began outlining a plan which seemed to amuse her more and more as she continued. Before she had finished speaking both she and Doris were laughing.

"Let's go and tell it to Miss Remson now," Doris proposed eagerly. She held out her hand to Muriel.

"The present is ours." Muriel blithely accepted the hand and away the two went. When they returned to their room almost an hour later they left Miss Remson smiling over the surprise she had in store for the Orchid Club.

For the next three days Julia and Mildred held long, concerned confabs regarding what Miss Remson intended to do about the petition. Her manner, when they had talked with her, had been impersonal. They argued it as a good sign, however, that she should have asked for three days in which to consider the matter.

"If she had been down on us for getting up the petition she would probably have exploded like a firecracker," Mildred declared to Julia on the afternoon of the second day as they came from Science Hall. "We may be doing her a favor by objecting to Miss Cairns. It may be that she disapproves of Miss Cairns, too, but has to walk softly because Prexy has shown such marked partiality in her case."

"Miss Remson likes Miss Cairns," differed Julia. "She makes quite a good deal of fuss over her. Of course, there is just a chance that she only pretends to like her on account of her father's money."

"The P. G.'s don't act as though they knew a thing about the petition," Mildred observed triumphantly. "They are too busy with plays and college welfare work to trouble themselves to watch us."

"It's a good thing. I'm glad Miss Dean isn't at the Hall now. Miss Remson would surely tell her about our petition. She is Miss Remson's pet. She used always to be stirring up things here and interfering in the girls' private affairs. Doris Monroe is the only one I am uncertain of. She is really Miss Cairns' friend. Let her hear a word of this business!" Julia paused impressively.

"Oh, she isn't so formidable. She dearly loves to swank. She is altogether too top-lofty to suit me." Mildred's face clouded. Doris's superior air was a great cross to her. "She poses with that white fur motor coat, and white car on purpose to keep herself before the campus."

"She knows better than to be top-lofty with me," Julia said in an independent tone. "I am the only girl on the campus who made her understand that I'd not fall down and worship her."

"Hm-m," was Mildred's sole response. It reminded Julia forcibly of Clara. Clara had signed the petition, but had secretly regretted the act. She was hourly growing more disgusted with Julia and frequently wondered how she had ever even believed she liked her quarrelsome roommate. She was no longer jealous of Mildred. She detested the bold freshman more than ever, and derived a resentful pleasure from the thought that Julia and Mildred could not possibly stay friends for any length of time.

On the morning of the third day Miss Remson called Julia and Mildred into her office from the breakfast table to inform them that she would meet the Orchid Club as a body in the living room that evening at eight o'clock to discuss with them the matter of the petition.

At half past seven Annie ushered Marjorie, winsome and smiling into the kitchen by way of the back door. "Miss Remson's in her sitting room watching for you, Miss Marjorie," she gigglingly announced. Annie was under the impression that a huge joke was to be played upon someone. She had no idea as to what it might be, or who was the victim. She merely giggled in sympathy.

Up in Miss Remson's room Marjorie found Leslie Cairns, Doris Monroe, Muriel Harding and the manager awaiting her arrival at the Hall. As she had spent the previous evening with them in the same sitting room she responded to her friends' laughingly significant greetings in the same spirit.

"Now girls," Miss Remson addressed the quartette in her bright fond fashion. "I leave the carrying out of the program to you. Keep in line behind me when the door is opened and I step into the living room. If objection to your presence at the meeting is made, let me talk to the objectors."

"We'll be silent as specters till it comes our turn to talk," Muriel assured, her velvety brown eyes twinkling her enjoyment of the occasion.

At precisely eight o'clock Miss Remson's doubled fist beat an imperative little tattoo on the living room door. A small blue-eyed freshman with a worried expression opened the door. She sent up an abashed "Oh!" and watched the line of five file into the room in amazed fascination. The manager led her companions straight up the aisle formed by the arrangement of rows of chairs, oblivious to the growing murmur of voices which attended her progress up the room. She paused near the two chairs set in an open space at the end of the room which were occupied by the president and vice-president of the Orchid Club. The four girls grouped themselves behind her. A dead stillness descended upon the room. It was an ominous stillness such as precedes a storm.

CHAPTER XXII.

THE WAY THE MEETING TURNED OUT

Suddenly the storm broke. A babel of protesting exclamations arose, growing louder. A tall sophomore with glasses sprang to her feet crying out: "This is not fair, Miss Remson. Our club is strictly private. No one except the members and yourself was invited to be here tonight. I object, Madame President." She whirled, appealing to Julia.

"Miss Saylor, your objection is sustained." Julia's expression was one of empty dignity. She looked ludicrously owl-like. "We are glad of Miss Remson's presence here tonight. However, we prefer not to have outsiders at our business meetings." She regarded the four "outsiders" with a cold stare. "Please take this chair, Miss Remson." She nodded to a vacant chair near her own.

"Thank you." Miss Remson seated herself without further remark.

The noise attending the entrance of Miss Remson and her four aides had partially subsided while Julia was speaking. It now began again. Half a dozen girls simultaneously found their feet to make displeased protest.

Suddenly Muriel stepped in front of her companions and raised a hand for silence. Her gesture was thoroughly good-humored. Her sparkling face was full of condescending geniality. "My, but you are an inhospitable crowd!" she declared. "You don't know what you are trying to do. You are trying to put me out of the show business. These are my three performers and this is our next stand. Have a heart!"

No one could be more irresistibly funny than Muriel when she chose. Laughter greeted her mock reproachful speech, rather half-hearted, but laughter, nevertheless. The ominous babel of displeased voices died down.

"Miss Harding!" Julia adopted a tone of deep affront. "Won't you please consider the privacy of this club and——"

"How can you?" Muriel looked grieved, then laughter chased away her pretended grief. "Have pity on a poor showman, and his exhibits. 'Remember the stranger within thy gates,'" she quoted affably, well aware of the sighing breath that rose from the company at the reminder of Hamilton's first tradition. "There's money in this business for me this evening. I always take up a collection after each performance. Why be haughty? Stay and see the show."

"Show! Show!" The sunny side of girl nature could not but respond to Muriel's nonsensical blandishments. Here and there among the group a frowning face was to be seen. The majority were longing for fun, however. And the majority ruled. Then, too, Muriel was extremely well liked.

The laughing cry of "Show" continued. Julia Peyton raised an imperious hand in an effort to fix attention upon herself. She addressed the crowd, but the crowd refused to listen to her. Muriel had won her point. She had also delivered a pertinent rebuke under cover of her gaiety.

"Assert yourself as president," Mildred Ferguson urged Julia in low stormy tones. She was furious at the unexpected intrusion. "What does Miss Remson think she is going to do, I wonder? She'll not honor the petition. That's certain. To bring Miss Cairns in here! She means to fight for her and make us a whole lot of trouble—if she can."

"Oh, those provoking girls!" Julia was ready to cry with chagrin. "They're letting Miss Harding make perfect geese of them. And all because she is funny, or thinks she is."

"She's funny enough," Mildred admitted sulkily. She turned to listen against her will to Muriel's flow of inimitable nonsense.

Muriel had ranged Marjorie, Leslie and Doris in a row and was now engaged in busily showing them off to the roomful of girls. She treated them as she might have a collection of bisque dolls. She moved their arms and hands about at will, took them by the shoulders, one after another, spun them round then posed them in a series of ridiculously stiff attitudes. She finally pretended to wind up a mechanism between Marjorie's shoulders and Marjorie came to life and sang Stevenson's "In Winter," in a thin childish voice. She met with a cordial reception.

Doris, when wound up, executed a graceful little dance which was heartily applauded. Leslie came last. She sang a verse of a French song with an artistry of expression and gesture that was a revelation to the audience who had gathered to condemn her. After she had finished and given a funny little exhibition of running down and becoming immobile again an odd silence reigned. It was shattered by a girl's voice from the back of the room. "Clever, bravo!" she cried. "Encore, encore!"

Next instant the room rang with cries of "Encore!" Muriel favored her audience with a Cheshire puss smile and laboriously wound up Leslie again. She sang the second verse with more clever gestures.

When Muriel could make herself heard she went on to announce that the performance would close with one verse of "Lightly row," sung by the "Great Little Three." Then she promised to press speech buttons in the backs of the trio's necks. The Great Little Three would then thank their audience for their attention.

Rather to her surprise this announcement also elicited approval. She had been afraid the girls would scent a lecture in her words and shy off from it. Instead cries of "Speech! Speech!" ascended.

"Thank you for your appreciation," Marjorie began in her own sweet tones as Muriel stepped back from pressing the speech button at the nape of her white neck. "We should feel so hurt if we thought you hadn't liked us. Though we seem only mechanical we have very sensitive feelings. We are glad if we have amused you and we hope you will always think as kindly of us as we think of you." Thus Marjorie's little speech ended.

Doris came next. She said with her soft, fascinating drawl: "As I am a dancing doll it is very hard for me to speak. So I will say only that I wish the Orchid Club may flourish long as one of Hamilton's most representative sororities, with truth, honor and justice for its motto."

"Rah, rah, rah, for the college beauty!" proposed someone. The cheers were given with a will. Doris smiled and bowed her thanks, looking as lovely as a veritable fairy-tale princess. The audience could no more help liking her for her beauty than they could help succumbing to Marjorie's charm.

Leslie's speech began in French. She made two or three droll remarks in the language, accompanying them by truly Gallic gestures of her hands and shrugs of her shoulders. She was a French scholar, having spoken it from early childhood. Ripples of laughter from her listeners testified as to their admiration for her cleverness.

Suddenly she dropped into English with a change of tone that brought forth a kind of united gasp from the rows of girls. "And now the show is over, and the play is played out," she said in a steady, resolute tone that somehow carried with it an unspoken determination toward courage of the true sort. "I have read your petition. I have read the list written by Dulcie Vale. Both are a waste of paper. You can neither make nor mar me. I am the only one to do either. I know this now. I learned it by failing to accomplish such injustices against others as those you have lately framed against me. Whatever you may have heard of me belongs to the past; not the present. I am here to do a certain thing which I have promised myself shall be done. I shall continue to live at the Hall because Miss Remson wishes me to do so. But for all I did when I was at Hamilton nearly three years ago which was against tradition and honor I am reaping in this one respect. To live at Wayland Hall is the greatest punishment for me that could be devised. So my advice to you tonight is to leave me to work out my own salvation. I promise not to trouble you." With a grave inclination of the head Leslie stepped back beside

Marjorie. Marjorie put out an arm and dropped it affectionately about Leslie's waist.

"I think it's too bad; shameful in us!" A pretty brown-eyed young woman had sprung to her feet with the contrite cry. "How could we have been so—so spitefully foolish? I shall cross my name off that petition. Miss Remson won't you please destroy both it and that list? How many are with me in this?" She waved a rallying hand to the buzzing company.

"I am. And I." A babel of "I's" was heard.

Julia Peyton jumped up to defend the losing fight. Her voice was drowned in the noise. Mildred Ferguson tried to make herself heard and met with defeat.

Muriel had forsaken her duties as showman and was animatedly talking to two or three girls nearest to where she stood. Doris had come up on Leslie's other side and had also put an arm around Leslie. Miss Remson sat watching the noisy company, a bright smile on her thin, kind face.

Muriel stepped up to her and asked an eager question. Miss Remson handed her a thin packet of folded papers. Muriel took them, then faced the company. She waved them energetically in air until she had attracted general attention to herself.

"This is my license to go into the show business," she cried laughingly. "I find I shall be too busy from now on to need it. Is there anyone here who would like to have it?"

"No, no, no!" came the emphatic protest. "Burn it up. Tear it up. Lose it in the furnace!" and plenty of other suggestions answered her mischievous inquiry.

"All right." Muriel cast a laughing glance at Julia Peyton who was looking the picture of impotent wrath. She caught the glance and turned her head haughtily away. "I have no matches," Muriel continued apologetically, "and the furnace isn't handy. Shall I?" She made a move as though to tear the papers in half.

"*Yes*." The welcome affirmation came with a shout.

"And we are all friends?" Muriel asked with sly geniality.

"*Yes*." Again the shout echoed through the big room.

"Very well." Muriel showed candid delight in tearing the papers intended to cause unhappiness into bits. "Please pardon us for having interrupted your meeting," she went on. "We are going now. Good night. If any of you are thinking of starting in the show business I can give you pointers. I might even decide to lend you my dolls. Good night."

She made a smiling move toward leaving the room. The three other girls and Miss Remson followed her. None of them had stepped half way down the aisle before they were hemmed in by a jubilant, chattering crowd. An impromptu reception started in the middle of the aisle. Leslie found half a dozen hands extended to clasp hers.

"Tell the girls if you can make them hear you that there are three big ginger cakes in the cake box, and that free lemonade is a feature of your show," Miss Remson told Muriel.

In the midst of the cheer that hailed this good news Julia and Mildred skirted one side of the room, keeping as far from the jolly crowd as they could. They reached the door and hurried away from the meeting they had planned with such unkind zest. It had turned out very differently from their expectation.

CHAPTER XXIII.

OUT OF THE PAST

As a result of Muriel's show Leslie Cairns found herself in better standing among her housemates than she had dreamed ever of attaining. It often takes some very small thing to turn the tide of approval or disapproval. The tide had turned in Leslie's favor when Muriel had quoted Hamilton's highest tradition. Hardly a girl present but that had experienced a secret twinge of conscience for the petition they had signed against Leslie Cairns.

Nor had it been particularly reassuring to see Marjorie Dean, Doris Monroe, Muriel Harding and Miss Remson firmly entrenched against them. While they counted as the majority at the Hall the Bertram girls and the post graduates were powers on the campus. At first Julia's and Mildred's strenuous objections to Leslie had made an impression upon their housemates. Dulcie Vale's despicable communication had bolstered their disapproval only at the time of hearing. Later, in thinking it over and talking together about it, the more serious element of the girls had cherished doubts as to its entire veracity. It was Julia's stanchest supporters who had started the objection when the four girls and Miss Remson had walked in upon their meeting. In the end even they had come shame-faced to a more charitable view of matters.

Doris had been touched to learn from Miss Remson that on the day of the meeting Clara Carter had come to her and asked to be permitted to strike her name from the petition. Meeting Clara face to face on the campus the day following the meeting Doris had shaken hands with the red-haired girl and invited her to dinner at Baretti's. Clara had accepted with surprised joy and had agreeably surprised Doris by her avoidance of personal gossip. Of Julia she said nothing. Nor did Doris mention Julia's name.

At Hamilton Arms Marjorie was beginning to look forward to the fruits of her planting. February was a triumphal month to her because toward the latter part of it she completed the biography of Brooke Hamilton. On the third Sunday in February she had completed her work except for a last paragraph which she had purposely left to be written on a special occasion. That Sunday having been chosen as the special occasion the original Travelers came to Hamilton Arms to spend the afternoon and evening. At five o'clock, the hour when Brooke Hamilton had welcomed tea in his workshop, a reverent little company gathered in the study. There, Marjorie, surrounded by her friends composed the final paragraph and triumphantly wrote "The End" at the bottom of the last page of manuscript. Then in turn the girls recited the Brooke Hamilton maxims and Miss Susanna read a prayer, a translation from the German, of which Brooke Hamilton had been fond. As a last tribute to him they had lifted up their fresh young voices in the Hymn to Hamilton, filling the departed founder's workshop with melody while he appeared to smile contentedly down from the wall at the sweet-voiced singers.

The manuscript for the biography was to be placed in the hands of a New York publisher. Marjorie's color deepened every time she happened to recall the fact that when the biography should have been published she would then be Marjorie Dean Macy.

"It is a relief to know the biography is done," she said to Miss Susanna on the morning after she had completed it in the presence of her intimates. "There are so many other things to think of. Next week the dormitory will be ready for the furniture. Then will come the dedication of it. After that will be the library dedication. Then we must have a house warming. It will take two weeks to place the furniture, and one week to celebrate. There are three whole weeks of March gone and from that on you know how it will be. Captain will be here, and I'll have to resign myself to innumerable fittings. Oh, dear!" Marjorie's sunny smile accompanied the half rueful exclamation.

"You are a much harrassed person." Miss Susanna's sympathy was too dry to be genuine. She smiled her crinkly smile at Marjorie and said: "Are you going to be very busy this morning. Marvelous Manager?"

"Very. I have an engagement with Miss Susanna Hamilton to do whatever she would like to have me do." Marjorie rose from where she had been sitting at the study table writing to her Captain and crossed to the small, bright-eyed figure in the doorway. She offered Miss Susanna both hands with the pretty impulsiveness that was one of her charms.

"Come then." Miss Susanna took Marjorie by the arm and began walking her gently down the long hall and toward her own spacious, airy bed room. It was a beautiful room with a big sunny bow window and handsome old-fashioned furnishings. There was a canopied four poster bed, high-backed mahogany chairs, with a highboy and immense dresser to match. A gate-legged table, high desk and several other notable antiques made up a collection which a dealer in antiques would have regarded with envious eyes.

From girlhood it had been Miss Susanna's room, and she had never allowed any change to be made in it from the way in which she had found it when she came to Hamilton Arms to live with her distinguished kinsman.

As she stepped over the threshold of her girlhood sanctum, clinging to Marjorie's arm, she steered the young girl across the room and brought her to a forced, playful halt before a very large black teakwood chest. It was purely Chinese in character, the lid being decorated with an intricate gold pattern, the spiral complicated curves of which emanated from the wide-open jaws of a gold dragon.

Marjorie had always greatly admired the chest. Once she had asked Miss Susanna if it had not been brought from China by Brooke Hamilton. The old lady had replied "Yes, my dear," with a peculiar brevity which Marjorie had early learned to recognize as a sign that Miss Hamilton preferred to close the subject before it had hardly been broached.

"I brought you here with me this morning, dear child, to show you something that belongs to the long ago. It's something I've often debated letting you see. I have decided as many times against it as for it. But after I knew that you were going to put a cranky old person named Hamilton in the seventh heaven of delight by getting married at the Arms, I knew I should show you this chest, and what's in it, and tell you the history of it. This is only for you, Marjorie. But you may tell your Captain, and Hal, for you must never have secrets from either your mother, or your husband."

"Then Mystified Manager said to Goldendede, the keeper of the castle, 'I will obey you in all things, Goldendede, for I know you to be a wise woman.'" Marjorie laughingly improvised. "That's the way I feel. The enchantment of the castle hangs over me, and I am on the way to marvelous revelations."

"Marvelous? I don't know." The old lady's head tilted to its bird-like angle. "I believe the only marvelous part is that I did not get married. Now perhaps you can guess what's in that chest." She eyed Marjorie shrewdly.

"Miss Susanna!" Light had suddenly dawned upon Marjorie. "You mean—" She stopped, then cried: "Was that chest your hope—"

"It was," came the crisp response. "In it is my wedding dress." She threw back the lid as she spoke, then removed a white linen cover arranged over the contents of the chest as a protection.

Marjorie gasped in girl admiration as she caught sight of fold upon fold of heavy pearl-seeded white satin. "Oh!" she exhaled rapturously. "How beautiful!"

Miss Susanna lifted the billows of satin from the box. "I'll lay out the dress on my bed." She gathered the creamy folds in her arms and trotted over to her bed. Looking in the box, Marjorie saw a teakwood tray that extended across the box. In it were a pair of long white gloves, a pair of the most exquisitely embroidered white silk stockings she had ever seen and an underslip of thin white Chinese silk embroidered in a pattern of orange blossoms. The stockings also bore the same pattern embroidered in a straight strip up and down the fronts.

"Bring over the accessories which I didn't need, child," Miss Susanna directed, matter-of-fact in the midst of reminders of her own romance.

Marjorie gathered up the lovely things and carried them over to the bed. As Miss Susanna had already walked toward the chest Marjorie laid the dainty articles of the bridal outfit reverently upon the snowy expanse of linen spread.

While she was engaged in the pleasant yet half sad task, Miss Susanna returned to her side. Her eyes directed toward the wedding gown, which was a dream of loveliness, she suddenly felt something falling down over her head and face in misty, transparent folds. She cried out and looked through the delicate transparency to see Miss Susanna smiling at her with untold tenderness.

"It was to have been my wedding veil, Marjorie. I wish it to be yours. Come over to the mirror and let me drape it on you. You are not much taller than I. Thank fortune this veil is yards and yards in length and width. The present-day veils are so very voluminous."

"This veil is a poem, Goldendede," Marjorie declared fervently; "a poem in pearls, mist and orange blossoms. Surely, there was never its equal on land or sea!"

She had obediently moved to the great oval mirror of the dresser, standing slim and lovely in her white lawn morning gown. Over her head and flowing down to her feet and far beyond them was the exquisite veil of finest Brussels net, outlined with pearls and caught up here and there with sprays of creamy satin orange blossoms which closely resembled the natural blossoms. The dainty bridal cap formed by the gathering together of the veil was banded with pearls and orange blossoms. Squarely in front and slightly below the pearl band was a star of matched pearls.

"Can this be I?" Marjorie cried jokingly, yet half embarrassed. The mirror told her the story of her own beauty so clearly she felt an unbidden desire to cry over the fact that she was beautiful in the marvelous veil. "Where did it come from, Goldendede?" she asked wonderingly. "It's not that I am beautiful. It's the veil. It could transform the plainest person from positive homeliness to beauty."

"It would go a long way toward it," Miss Susanna smiled indulgently at the enchanting vision before the mirror. "Still, I must say that I never looked as you do in it, child. And I was a fairly pretty girl, too. Uncle Brooke and I made a voyage to Europe on purpose to order my trousseau. He bought the most expensive piece of net for sale in Brussels. We took it to Paris and had the veil made there with the rest of the trousseau. That is the history of it."

The old lady stood back to view the effect of the veil upon Marjorie, an absent, meditative look in her bright eyes.

"The days that followed the breaking of my engagement with Gray were hard; hard indeed," she continued. "His name was Grayson Landor. He was very good-looking. But he did not love me; nor I him. He knew it when he proposed marriage to me. I did not know until after I had steeled myself against seeing him. He was unworthy, child; utterly unworthy. He was in love with a poor young girl, really in love with her, yet he was content to forsake her and marry me for my money, and because I was a Hamilton. I am glad I found him out in time. I realize more and more that I was chosen to carry on Uncle Brooke's plans, and alone. I regret the years I lost through Alec Carden's interference."

The mistress of the Arms sat down on the edge of a chair and folded her hands together. "Yes; I lost so much time," she said musingly, almost as though she had forgotten Marjorie's presence.

"Why did I name you Goldendede?" Marjorie demanded with severity. "What about the dormitory site, and the Brooke Hamilton Library and the biography, and your general generousness to Hamilton? Even when you felt resentment against Hamilton you tried to carry out his wishes so far as the business part of the college was concerned. Many persons placed in the same circumstances would have refused to continue the endowment which Mr. Brooke made Hamilton, but subject to your approval after his death. You were truly chosen to carry out his plans. I always feel that somewhere in eternity Mr. Brooke knows and is glad."

CHAPTER XXIV.

LOVE YOUR ENEMIES

True to Marjorie's prediction one momentous event after another, relative to her many campus interests, caused March to skim away on wings. On the fifth day of March, which fell upon Saturday, Hamilton College turned out in full force to attend the dedication of the dormitory. Due to the large crowd that must inevitably be present the exercises had been scheduled to take place in the open air in the large open space in front of the building. In the event of bad weather they would be conducted in the assembly hall of the building. It was hoped by the Travelers that the day for which they had toiled so faithfully would be mild and sunny.

When the day came it proved to be a marvel of balmy breezes and warm sunshine. It was one of those rare early spring days which promise so smilingly of the return of Spring in her glory.

The dedication exercises began at one o'clock before the largest student body ever enrolled at Hamilton College and in charge of the Reverend Compton Greene, the oldest minister in the county of Hamilton, and also the Episcopal minister at Hamilton Estates. A platform had been erected as a speakers' stand. On the platform sat President Matthews, the members of the Hamilton College Board, Miss Susanna, Peter Graham, Professor Venderblatt, Miss Remson, Signor Baretti, Marjorie, Robin and the other eight members of the original Travelers' Chapter. The two new chapters of Travelers attended the dedication in a body, occupying a special place on the lawn roped off for them.

The faculty also attended in a body, grouped well to the right of the speakers' stand. To the left stood row upon row of dark-faced men dressed in their best, their faces bright with smiles. Their leader, Peter Graham had Signor Baretti on one side of him and on the other a tall, broad-shouldered man with keen dark eyes and a firm mouth. Peter Cairns had demurred at accepting the honor of standing with Peter Graham on such an occasion. "Oh, I'll stay at the edge of the crowd," he had declared, but had been overruled by his two friends.

"You don't come and make the strike break up, and my countrymen go work like these should, we don't have any dorm now. So you help, too, and you should go with us. Why you are ashamed to be seen with us? I am once poor Italiano, but very respec'bl," had been the argument Baretti had used to Mr. Cairns. He had finally won his point.

Among the company of Travelers in the roped-in space was Leslie Cairns. She had also yielded to persuasion, though she had still the humiliated inner conviction that she did not deserve such kindness on the part of the Travelers.

Marjorie, Robin and Miss Susanna had all vowed firmly before hand that under no circumstances would they be drawn into speech making. "Let the men make the speeches," Miss Susanna had said with an emphatic nod. The uneasy partners had agreed with her and informed her that they should depend upon her to stick to her guns.

When the time came, however, Miss Susanna found herself the center of a student body, ready to bow down to her. She received an ovation that amazed her to the point of all but reducing her to tears. Sturdy soul that she was she set her jaws and refused to break down. She had to make a speech, however, and the few terse sentences she spoke came straight from her heart.

Neither were Page and Dean permitted "to get by" without a speech. Robin came first and spoke with the charming sincerity which was the keynote of her disposition. Marjorie listened to her in active discomfort, all too sure that she would be called upon next. She tried to think of something to say, but her mind suddenly seemed to become blank.

Worried over her own lack of inspiration she scarcely heard what Robin said. She merely caught the tones of her partner's earnest voice. Presently Robin had finished speaking and applause broke out in deafening waves. After a little it subsided. Then—Marjorie heard President Matthews announce her to the acclaiming throng. As she rose it came to her that there was one subject on which she could speak—the greatness of Brooke Hamilton. There were so many wonderful things to be said of him.

She began her speech with: "Dear friends of Hamilton College.... Because Mr. Brooke Hamilton adored and venerated his mother, because he wished the highest for womankind, we are here today to do him honor by adding our bit to the splendid educational plans he made and carried out so nobly in the building of Hamilton College." Her voice, clear and ringing, carried to the farthest limits of the enthusiastic throng.

Brooke Hamilton could have had no stauncher advocate than Marjorie. In the short speech she made she brought before the assembled company the man as she had come to know him through her work on his biography. She ended eloquently with:

"When his biography is given to the world he will take his rightful place among the great men who have devoted their lives to aiding the cause of education. He planned unselfishly, and gave royally. He must be to us who love our Alma Mater the great example. Because we have believed in his maxims we shall try to live by them."

She was surprised when she resumed her chair next to Jerry to find her eyes full of tears. She had been carried away by the very earnestness of her praise for the founder of Hamilton.

"Pretty fair, Bean; pretty fair," was the welcome whisper from Jerry, which threatened to upset her gravity. "You done noble."

"*Taisez vous*, Jeremiah. I almost cried. Now please don't make me laugh. I'm glad it's all over. I never was intended as a speechifier."

"You only think you weren't, Bean, dear Bean. 'Speechifier's' a fine word; I shall adopt it. I'm sure it isn't in the 'dic.' That's what I'm looking for, original words; like 'celostrous,' for instance."

Satisfied to have made Marjorie laugh Jerry subsided. Presently a final prayer was said by the Reverend Greene, and the large company joined in the singing of the Doxology. Following the exercises the enthusiastic throng moved forward to inspect the new dormitory, the massive entrance doors of which stood open as though inviting visitors.

Among the few students who did not follow the crowd were Julia Peyton and Mildred Ferguson. Mildred was frankly contemptuous over the whole affair. She was not interested in a dormitory for the use of needy students, nor did she care anything about Brooke Hamilton as the founder of the college.

"Shucks," she commented disdainfully to Julia as the two turned away from the animated scene. "Let's go back to the campus. Somebody had to found Hamilton. Why should there be so much fuss made over it?"

"That small woman on the platform!" Julia exclaimed in consternation. "That was Miss Susanna Hamilton! I saw her at the Hall and thought she was Miss Remson's sister."

"Well, she doesn't know it," shrugged Mildred.

Julia, however, was anything but at ease in mind. Ever since the dismal failure of the attempt to force Leslie Cairns from Wayland Hall she had been more or less gloomy and morose. She had haughtily declared on the day after Muriel's "show" that she would not any longer keep the presidency of the club. She would not even attend any future meetings. She wrote a resignation as president and intrusted it to Mildred to read to the club.

Mildred read it out to the members at the next meeting of the Orchid Club. It was accepted with such alacrity, and a new president so promptly elected, that she decided she would not be so foolish as risk her membership in the club by offering to resign. She was inwardly peeved in that she had not been appointed president and another girl elected as vice-president. Only her ability to brazen things out kept her in a club in which the attitude of its other members toward her was one of polite endurance.

Julia's club troubles were less to her, however, than Clara Carter's defection. Clara still roomed with her, but paid very little attention to her. The red-haired girl was trying to model her acts on a higher basis. She was completely out of sympathy with her former intimate.

Julia also had another worry which had at first seemed too remote for anxiety. Her mother had written her that her father had met with severe losses in his manipulations of stocks. She had paid little attention to this news from home. Her father frequently engaged in the daring raids on the market which had earned him the name of "Wolf Peyton." Later, her mother had written her again of her father's critical financial situation. This time Julia had heeded the alarm of her mother's sounding. She knew it to be serious from the very fact that her mother had written her twice on the subject.

The day after the dedication of the dormitory she received a third letter from home that sent her into a panic. She let it overcome her to the extent of cutting her classes for the day and staying in her room to weep dismally over the Peytons' changed prospects.

"What is the matter?" Clara Carter asked Julia not unsympathetically as she came in from her Greek recitation to find Julia seated lachrymosely in the very chair she had been occupying when Clara had left their room.

"Nothing," Julia gulped, and sighed.

"There certainly must be. You hardly ever cry."

"You wouldn't be interested to know if I tell you," Julia quavered. "You are not my friend any more."

"I would be if you would try to do as you should," Clara returned with stolid dignity. "I don't care much about you lately, Julia, but I used to like you. Only both of us were wrong in the way we gossiped about the girls. We used to wonder sometimes why Doris was so queer and haughty with us at times. I know now that it was because she disapproved of our gossiping. Now when I am with her I never say an unkind word about anyone. And she is sweet to me on that very account."

"I wish I had never got up that miserable petition, or listened to a word Mildred Ferguson told to me about that Dulcie Vale, her cousin," Julia's voice rose to a disconsolate wail.

"I am very glad I came to my senses in time and had my name taken off the list," Clara returned grimly. "I feel sorry for you, somehow, Julia, though you've only yourself to blame for what's happened." Clara had not yet reached a point of forbearance wherein she could honestly sympathize with her roommate. She had not yet arrived at the charitable spirit of which she now gave signs of someday achieving.

"I know it." Julia held her handkerchief to her eyes, continuing to cry softly.

"I'd truly like to know what troubles you, Julia," Clara presently said in a softer tone than she had at first used.

"I can't come back to Hamilton next year," Julia sobbed out. "We've lost our money; everything we own, too. My father has been having bad luck in the market for the past year. My mother knew he was losing, but didn't think things were so bad as they've just turned out to be. We are poor, terribly poor. I am going to stay here the rest of this year, but I can't come back next year. My father says I'll have to become his secretary, and he'll have only a small office. It will take him quite a while to get over this failure and we'll have to live in a common three story house, and maybe not have even one car. Mother says we will try to keep my car for her use. It's all so terrible. I was never poor. I can't bear to think about it. And I want to come back to Hamilton for my senior year more than anything."

"Why don't you come back and live at the dormitory? Your father could afford to pay your fees, couldn't he?" Clara suggested. This time she showed real sympathy.

"No. That is I'm not sure. It's his idea—for me to be his secretary. He says I've always been so wasteful and extravagant that it is time I had to shoulder a little responsibility. He'd have to pay a confidential secretary capable of doing his work not less than from fifty to a hundred dollars a month. He says he must cut expenses to a minimum in order to pull himself up again financially. It may take him a year to do it. He made my mother write me all this. She is dreadfully upset by the whole thing. Anyway I wouldn't come back to the campus as a dormitory girl. I simply *couldn't*!" Julia exclaimed vehemently.

"My father would lend your father some money, Julia, if I were to ask him," Clara said after a short silence, broken only by the sound of Julia's muffled sobs.

"No, no." Julia made a dissenting gesture. "My father is awfully proud. He wouldn't accept help from even his oldest friends. He's an out and out crank about such things. Thank you just the same, Clara. It's sweet in you to wish to help me. I—I—appreciate—it. Never mind me. You'd better hurry along, or you'll be late for French."

Clara cast a hasty glance at the wall clock, gathered up her books and hurried away. On her way to her recitation she racked her brain for some way in which she might help Julia. Of the Wall Street realm of financiering she knew very little. Her father was a manufacturer and had inherited wealth from his father. Julia had occasionally told her tales of "Wolf" Peyton's exploits as a financier. She had never been much interested in hearing them. She now wished she had listened to them more attentively.

Her mind fixed on the subject of Julia's misfortunes, she paid little attention to her French lesson. On the way back to Wayland Hall she chanced to encounter Doris Monroe.

"What are you looking so solemn about, Clara?" Doris greeted in friendly fashion.

"Oh, I was just thinking. Somebody just told me some bad news. Not about myself," she added quickly. "I was just trying to think of a way I could help the person."

"Is there anything I can do?" Doris' alert brain instantly reverted to Julia Peyton. She had caught a glimpse of Julia hurrying through the hall to her room that morning and had noticed her woebegone expression.

"No. Why, I don't know." Clara paused uncertainly. "I'd be breaking a confidence to tell you, but you might know of a way to help."

"I'd rather you wouldn't break a confidence," Doris returned candidly.

"I know. But—" Clara hesitated again, "—I think I could tell you of the difficulty without naming the person. It would do no harm, Doris, I can assure you of that."

"I'll take your word for it," Doris made quick response.

Clara colored with pleasure. Doris's confidence in her was gratifying. "The father of a certain student here has lost all his money. He is a Wall Street financier. He is going to be awfully poor for a while. This student I speak of will not be able to come back to Hamilton next year. Her father says she will have to be his secretary. She feels very badly about it. She'd like to complete her college course. I wish I knew a way to help her father financially. I told her that my father would lend her father some money, but she said he would not accept a loan from even a friend. I can't think of any other way to help. Can you?"

"No; not this minute. But I will think it over. Perhaps I may hit upon a brilliant idea. I'll see you tonight about it. Come to my room. We'll have more time to talk things over. I must run along." With a little farewell gesture Doris turned and ran toward Hamilton Hall, where she would make her next recitation.

While Clara continued to ponder the matter without success it haunted Doris, also. She was now positive that the student in question was Julia Peyton. She had heard that Julia's father was a Wall Street "raider." Leslie Cairns had gone to some pains to explain the term to her. Leslie—of course! The very one to know what should be done. Thought of Julia's despicable part in the recent plot against Leslie's welfare recurred to Doris. Leslie could hardly be blamed if she refused to consider helping Julia. Leslie, however, understood a great deal about the world in which her father had piled up millions. Doris decided with her usual calm judgment that Leslie should be in her room that evening when Clara came to it. Muriel would be away at the rehearsal of a play which Leila was directing. She would ask Clara in Leslie's presence to tell Leslie what the red-haired girl had just told her.

When Clara stepped into Doris's room that evening she cast an unconsciously disappointed look at Doris. She had not expected to see Leslie Cairns. Doris caught the glance, understood it and said instantly:

"Please don't mind Leslie's being here, Clara. I asked her to come. I wish you to tell her what you told me this morning. Her father is one of the greatest financiers in the United States, or in Europe, perhaps. Leslie knows a great deal about finance. She will surely find a way to help you."

"I—I—you couldn't help in this affair, Miss Cairns," Clara burst forth in embarrassment. "It wouldn't be possible for you to."

"Why not?" Leslie turned a direct kindly glance upon the red-haired girl. "Please tell me. I know nothing of what it may be. I do know that I'd like to be of service. I have several years of pleasing no one but myself to make up for." She smiled her grimly humorous smile.

It took a little more coaxing, however, before Clara would yield. Finally she did so, telling Leslie what she had previously told Doris. Leslie listened without comment, until Clara had wound up her doleful little tale. She sat with one elbow on an arm of her chair, one hand cupping her chin.

"I think my father can find the way to help this man," she said reassuringly. "Pardon me when I say I believe I know who this man is. I have heard of him often from my father." She paused, viewing Clara with mute inquiry.

Clara understood. "I—I—it's Julia's father," she stammered. "Perhaps I should not have told you his name. Julia did not ask me not to. But she gave me her confidence. It—"

"It was necessary for me to know," Leslie cut in with a trace of her old-time brusqueness. "How can my father help a man regain his financial ground unless he knows that man's identity?" she asked half humorously.

"Well, of course not." Clara brightened, laughing a little.

"Will you trust the matter to me for a few days, perhaps weeks, Miss Carter?" Leslie asked kindly. "I will write to my father at once. Meanwhile the matter shall be one of strict confidence among us three. I should prefer Miss Peyton never to know the source from which help came to her father through any of us. I believe my father may wish not to be known in the matter, either."

"You speak with great confidence, Miss Cairns. You are sure something can be done by your father for Mr. Peyton?" Clara asked half doubtfully.

"Very sure," Leslie repeated encouragingly.

Clara did not remain in Doris's room long. She went back to her own room to find Julia making a conscientious effort to study.

"I mustn't neglect what last few opportunities I have," she said soberly. "I shall try to do well in all my subjects for the rest of the year."

"That's a brave view to take." Clara longed to tell Julia what she had just done. She smiled to herself. The more she considered Leslie's quiet confidence in her father's success the more she was inclined herself to believe in it.

In her room Leslie had just finished a brief but forceful letter to her father. It read:

> "DEAR PETER THE GREAT:
>
> "Here is a further chance for you to prove your greatness. Do you know a raider on the Street named Wolf Peyton? Of course you do. You know them all. He has lost his fortune. Dead broke. His daughter expects nothing but to leave college this June. She must come back for her senior year. It seems he needs her as his secretary, or thinks he does. I think the secretary business would flivver after he had tried it. Anyhow please put him on his feet so it won't be necessary for her to sacrifice her senior year. He may be your bitterest enemy, his daughter thought she was mine, but, never mind. We should tremble. Fix it up without him knowing you did anything.
>
> "I am going to be in one of Page and Dean's shows. It is to be a revue, and will be given on the evening of the eighth of April. You had better come to it. I am going to sing a French song and give some of those funny imitations of Parisians which

you like to see me do. I am happy, Peter. The Hedge begins to look like a near future proposition. With oceans of love. I'll write again soon.

"Faithfully,

"LESLIE."

CHAPTER XXV.

THE REWARD OF COURAGE

Ten days later Julia Peyton gloomily opened a letter from home and read in it news as surprisingly joyful as the news she had formerly received from home had been full of trouble. Her mother wrote that her father had managed somehow to tide over his losses and was on his financial feet again.

Clara shared the good news with Julia and privately Doris and Leslie shared it with Clara. As a result of Leslie's little "flier" in human happiness Doris made a special luncheon engagement with Marjorie Dean on purpose to confide to Marjorie what Leslie had done. Marjorie in turn confided the story of the girl who had obeyed the command of Christ, "Love your enemies," to the letter.

"She deserves a citation," was Miss Susanna's hearty opinion. "I will have a maxim hung for her at the college. Peter Carden and I will go over to chapel together that morning. She is a dear courageous child and deserves to be honored. That will put her on a splendid basis on the campus and she will have won the right to have her father named as the giver of the Leila Harper Playhouse."

"And we can have the presentation of the theatre to Leila made in the chapel during Commencement week," Marjorie planned joyously. "The theatre will be completed then. Mr. Graham said yesterday that he hoped to have it ready not later than the twentieth of June. You see, Goldendede, Hal has promised that we shall come down from our camp in the Adirondacks for Commencement at Hamilton."

"It is a good thing he has promised that you shall." Miss Susanna put on a mildly threatening air which vanished in a smile.

"Which motto are you going to give Leslie, Goldendede?" Marjorie inquired interestedly. The two fond comrades were strolling about the grounds of the Arms in the early spring sunshine.

"I'll let you choose."

"Then I know exactly the one I'd like for Leslie. It suits her so well. I mean the way she has tried this year on the campus to be a credit in all ways to her Alma Mater. The motto I'd like for her is the single one that hangs over near the portrait of him: 'A truly great soul is never dismayed.'"

"I wondered if you would choose that. It is in my mind, too, for her, Marvelous Manager. We had better have the citation this week so that Leslie may have that much longer to enjoy her glory on the campus. Saturday afternoon I think we'd better give a luncheon for her at the Arms and invite the three chapters of Travelers."

"You are always planning happiness for someone, dearest Lady of the Arms. Let's have Leslie here to tea this afternoon and make a fuss over her. We're not supposed to know about what she did for Julia Peyton. Wait until after the citation. Then I am going to tell her quietly that she has been found out," Marjorie declared, her eyes dancing.

"You are always planning happiness for someone, Marvelous Manager." Miss Susanna gave a fond imitation of Marjorie's tone.

"Oh, you!" Marjorie made one of her usual merry rushes at the old lady and the pair hugged each other with a will. Both were supremely happy over the way Leslie Cairns had turned out.

"All this means that I'll soon have Peter as my next-door neighbor," the mistress of the Arms exhibited the utmost satisfaction at the prospect. "Peter has turned out to be a man worth while; a man in a hundred thousand. Perhaps I shall have him teach me the finance game," she added, jokingly. "At least he and Leslie will be good company."

Undreaming of the honor in store for her, Leslie walked into chapel on the following Friday morning after Marjorie's talk with Miss Susanna and met with a surprise which made her gasp. Up in front with President Matthews, who it seemed was to conduct the services that morning, sat her father and Miss Susanna. Why Peter the Great should be there she could not guess. She could only surmise that he and Miss Hamilton had been invited to the morning exercises by Prexy.

She saw her father's keen dark eyes search the rows of young women until he had found her. Their eyes met and the smile of comradeship which passed between them was a beautiful thing to see. It thrilled Leslie with a pride in herself which before that morning she had hardly dared recognize. Peter the Great need no longer be ashamed of her. She had tried to redeem her past offenses and she had not failed entirely. She had discovered in the methodical living over of her senior year at Hamilton that she was, after all, a person of small consequence. She had long since discarded her belief in money as power. She knew from her own earnest efforts in the right direction that work alone counted. It was not she personally who mattered. It was the earnest spirit within that was to be considered.

When, presently, Doctor Matthews announced that three citations were on the program of the morning exercises Leslie immediately jumped to the conclusion that Barbara Severn and Phyllis Moore were to be honored. She generously hoped that Doris Monroe might be the third student for the honor. Doris was so charming to her fellow students. She had changed from indifferently proud to calmly sympathetic in the past year, and was rapidly coming to be liked as much for her graciousness as she had formerly been admired for her beauty.

"The maxims which Miss Susanna Hamilton has chosen to hang in various parts of Hamilton College in honor of the three young women she has chosen as deserving of a citation are maxims by Brooke Hamilton, framed and hung separately about his historic home, Hamilton Arms." President Matthews gave out the information to a breathlessly interested chapel full of girls.

Then Phyllis Moore was asked by him to rise. After he had accorded her a friendly commendation which made her cheeks burn he quoted the maxim to be hung in her honor, at the same time stating the place at Hamilton which it would occupy. It was: "Harmony followed in her footsteps." As a last touch he added: "This maxim was hung by Brooke Hamilton in his study as a tribute to Miss Angela Vernon, his fiancee, who died shortly before the date set for her marriage to Mr. Hamilton."

Barbara's maxim was "A merry heart doeth good like a medicine," and she was particularly complimented upon her sunny outlook on life.

As the applause attending Barbara's citation died out, Leslie listened eagerly for the name of the third student. She could not believe the evidence of her own ears when she heard Doctor Matthews requesting her to rise, then continuing:

"It is with great pleasure that I name Miss Leslie Cairns as the third student to have earned a citation. In our opinion Miss Hamilton has made a singularly happy choice of maxim." Then he quoted the motto Miss Susanna and Marjorie had chosen: "A truly great soul is never dismayed."

As she stood listening in stupefaction to the announcement she could see in all the chapel nothing but her father's face. He was smiling at her with a light in his dark eyes that repaid her a thousand times over for the effort she had made toward restitution. She was ready to break down and weep unrestrainedly. Nevertheless she did not. She controlled herself with an effort and received the honor as a true daughter of Peter Cairns might be counted upon to do. What amazed her, even more than the citation, was the tumultuous applause which broke out as she resumed her seat.

After the chapel the students held an impromptu reception outside the chapel in which she and Phil and Barbara were the center of an admiring and congratulatory crowd. Leslie had already clasped hands with her father and had heard his hearty: "Good work, Cairns II." It was the only commendation she craved.

"You are to be at Wayland Hall this afternoon at four o'clock," Muriel informed her as she shook hands vigorously with Leslie. "I am going to conduct a citation there for the benefit of Jeremiah Macy. She is in line for honors, too. She doesn't know it yet. It is up to Marjorie to drag her to the scene on time."

That Marjorie succeeded in dragging Jerry to Muriel's room was apparent that afternoon. At precisely four o'clock she marched her into the midst of a giggling throng of girls who were awaiting her arrival in exuberant spirits.

"What is the matter with you girls?" she demanded as she glanced comically from one to another of the laughing company. "What sort of joke do you think you are going to play on me?"

"It isn't a joke, Jeremiah, that we have in store for you," Ronny assured in a soothing tone. "You are in line for a citation; a very great honor, you know."

"No. I don't know. I can guess just about how great an honor it will be," Jerry retorted suspiciously.

"You are going to know this instant, Jeremiah. Vera is ready and waiting to laud and praise you. Now, Vera." Ronny made an impressive signal to Vera.

Vera came forward, bearing in her hands a medium-sized square book, thin as to pages and bound in soft dark blue leather. On the outside of the cover was printed in gold lettering the pertinent title: "Jingles to Bean. By Jeremiah Macy."

Vera thereupon began a speech which was drowned by laughter most of the time during the utterance. She concluded the presentation speech by opening the book and proudly disclosing to Jerry a kodak photograph of Jerry in the act of reciting a jingle. She was even shown with her mouth open and one hand out in a flamboyant gesture.

"How did you ever manage to catch me?" was Jerry's wondering query after she had laughed over the little book, which contained as many of the Bean jingles as the girls had been able to gather at the time when Jerry had improvised them.

"It was that afternoon on the campus when Leila had her camera and was taking pictures of the campus. She went out with it and you, on purpose. She planned with Marjorie to come over to the campus unexpectedly."

"Do not you remember I said to you, 'Since you are so glad to see Beauty then why do you not spout a jingle'!" Leila broke in, laughing. "While you were spouting it Vera walked off a little way with the camera and snapped the picture of our Jeremiah at the height of inspiration."

"Yes, I remember now. You crafty things!" Jerry pretended disapproval for a brief second. "It's celostrous," she said. "I'd rather have it than even a citation in chapel. But I've had that. I'm really embarrassed with riches. I shall keep my Bean Jingle Book as my most precious possession. I shall—"

"Put it on your parlor table when you become Mrs. Daniel Seabrooke," Muriel slyly supplemented.

"Who told you? Oh-h!" Jerry clapped a hand to her lips.

It was too late. She was surrounded by a buzzing, laughing, congratulatory mob.

Ronny stood back a little from the group watching the tumultuous reception of Jeremiah's news with an odd little smile. She was wondering what her friends would say if they knew a certain dear secret of which she had been in wondering possession only a few days. Ronny had fulfilled Marjorie's prediction. She had tumbled into love and with the last person she had dreamed she might come to care for.

Due to her love of dancing she had willingly consented to help Professor Leonard with his work as physical instructor at Hamilton by taking a class in folk dancing. Through her association with him she had learned to know and care for him. She had not believed, however, that he cared for her. Naturally secretive, she had never by a shade of tone or expression betrayed her secret to anyone. She had been deeply incensed with herself for having yielded to love in the least.

Then had come an afternoon when they two had been deep in planning the usual May Day procession on the campus. She had never known just how it all happened, except that he had told her the story of his early life. His mother, who had died in his boyhood, had been a Spanish Mexican. His father, a professor in a Mexican university, had been an American. From them he had inherited a desire to help the poor of the country of his birth. His one dream was to place himself financially in position where he might some day go about the welfare work of his heart. It would take years of self-denial and economy, but he was willing to work and wait.

Then he had told Ronny he loved her, but would not ask her to live a life of privation with him. Ronny had said that nothing in the world except love mattered. So they had sworn faith to each other. Privately Ronny was possessed of a certain knowledge which would make the way clear. It had long been her father's dream to establish a welfare station in Mexico by the planting of a great fruit ranch upon which the unfortunate, poverty-stricken Mexican peons might find work the year round at living wages. What Mr. Lynne wished most was the right man to put in charge of the proposed vast charitable enterprise. Ronny had regarded the idea as one which might become her life work. Now she knew that it would be, but that she would not go to it alone.

Thus the Sanford five who had so gayly entered into the land of college had all found love and betrothal except Lucy Warner. It was hanging over sedate Lucy, however. And in the time of June and roses she was to hear the old, old story from the only young man with whom she had ever managed to feel on easy terms. Lucy was destined some day to acknowledge dignified President Matthews as father-in-law.

CHAPTER XXVI.

MARJORIE DEAN MACY

"Have you any orders for me, Captain?" Marjorie Dean turned from the full-length wall mirror, both hands held out to her mother.

"None, Lieutenant, except the instruction, be happy." Mrs. Dean caught the slim, outstretched hands in hers and drew the beautiful vision in white brocade into her arms.

"Dearest child. I am so happy that this day has come for you." she murmured. "We are favored by God, darling, in that General and I are not going to be called to give you up. We shall still be with you, only we shall have gained a dear son."

"That is the most beautiful part of it all, Captain. I can never love Hal enough for wishing and arranging things so gloriously for us all."

"I mustn't embrace you to the extent of wrinkling your wedding gown," her mother said half tremulously, as she held Marjorie off from her and rejoiced in her loveliness.

"That doesn't make the least bit of difference." Marjorie wrapped her arms about her mother afresh and hugged her hard.

Her wedding gown was a marvel in a silvery white brocade satin. It was sleeveless and its simple artistic lines clung lovingly to her girlish slenderness. Around her neck was the string of pearls which her Sanford friends had given her at the party held in her honor at Gray Gables on the evening before she had started for Hamilton College as a freshman.

Pinned to the front of her pearl-trimmed corsage was a diamond star, Hal's wedding gift to her. It held in place a tiny knot of purple sweet-scented violets, from Brooke Hamilton's garden. The misty fall of her veil about her lovely face brought out its beauty anew. Never, even as the violet girl, would Marjorie Dean appear more beautiful.

As she stood affectionately clasping her mother in the last few moments left her as Marjorie Dean she was feeling that life had been almost too perfect to her. The crowning happiness had come to her within the past few days. Unbeknown to her Hal had purchased the Clements' estate across the pike from Hamilton Arms. There he and she would settle after their short honeymoon at his camp in the Adirondacks, and with them were to live General and Captain. Danny Seabrooke had purchased Castle Dean, and he and Jerry were to live in it when they should be married the following September.

For a week prior to the wedding Hamilton Arms had been in a state of dignified upheaval. The marriage ceremony of Hal and Marjorie was to be performed by the Reverend Compton Greene at sunset. The great drawing room doors leading into a long back parlor had been removed, leaving a space almost as large as that of a church. No place could have been more ideally suited to the violet wedding which Marjorie had wished for. At the end of the long back parlor was a small balcony. On it were to be Constance Stevens, Harriet Delaney, Robin Page, Blanche Scott, Phyllis Moore and Charlie Stevens. These last two were to play the obligatos for the singers. All her dear friends far and near had been invited to the ceremony, and the entire student body of Hamilton to the reception to follow.

Vera Mason and Barbara Severn had been chosen by Marjorie as flower girls on account of their diminutive stature. It was Marjorie's idea to have as many of her chums as possible figure in the wedding ceremony. Ronny was to be the ring bearer. Jerry her maid of honor. The bridesmaids were to be Leila Harper, Leslie Cairns, Helen Trent, Muriel Harding, Lucy Warner and Doris Monroe.

She had studied long and patiently for a way to include the remaining Travelers of her chapter and those of the other two chapters, as well as the Bertram group of girls. Finally inspiration had hit upon a plan beautifully in keeping with her desire for a violet wedding. In pursuance of it she had gathered her chums, as well as the girls who were to take part in her plan, at Hamilton Arms, the day before the wedding. There a merry afternoon had been spent picking the long-stemmed purple single violets that grew in profusion in the meadow behind the Arms.

Each girl had gathered her own immense bouquet of violets, which she would carry at the wedding. Dressed in white they would form an aisle between which the bridal party would walk down the room to the altar. Each girl holding her violets, fastened with graceful streamers of pale violet ribbon.

Now the last plan had been carried out. Downstairs an eager company was seated on each side of the broad ribbon-enclosed aisle, awaiting the arrival of the bride.

Came a gentle knock on the door. In response to Marjorie's "Come," Miss Susanna entered, a distinguished little figure in her dull silver lace frock.

"I only came up for a last minute with Marjorie Dean," she said. She took Marjorie very gently in her arms. "I wish you and Captain to come with me," was her crisp request, after she and Marjorie had indulged in one of their hearty embraces.

She led them down the hall to her room. As they entered both Marjorie's and her mother's eyes were attracted to a new object in the room. It was a chest of some sort of creamy white rare wood polished to a high degree. On the lid and sides were painted exquisite clusters of double purple violets.

"This is Brooke Hamilton's wedding present to you, child." Miss Susanna's brisk tones faltered a trifle. "It was Angela Vernon's hope chest which he brought her from the far East. I could not find it in my heart to place it downstairs with your other gifts. It is only for us. And now I will say, too, that when I shall have passed on to the brightness of beyond, Hamilton Arms and all it entails will be yours. I shall always feel that Uncle Brooke knew and sent you to me, so that you may carry on the work of loving and preserving Hamilton College unto the perfect end after I shall have finished my part of it."

Five minutes later Marjorie was smiling again after a sudden little tear shower that she had not tried to control. Then Miss Susanna and her captain left her, and her throng of pretty wedding attendants gathered in the upstairs hall for the formation to the altar. Jerry was looking her prettiest in her gown of pale violet chiffon and a huge bouquet of violets and orchids. It was to be a hatless wedding. The bridesmaids were in orchid colored chiffon growns, each carrying a sheaf of white and purple lilacs. Ronny, as ring-bearer wore a marvelous gown of white gold-embroidered tissue. Robin and Barbara, as flower girls, wore crystal-beaded chiffon gowns of palest lavender and carried artistic long-handled baskets filled with white and purple sweet-scented violets.

The procession formed in anything but a stately manner. There was a great deal of fond laughing and talking, as the girls fluttered into place. First went the advance guard of white. They descended the stairs two by two, separating at the wide entrance doorway leading into the drawing room and taking their places inside the two stretches of broad violet satin ribbon.

Waiting only until the advance guard had formed below stairs, the bridesmaids led the way on Marjorie Dean's most momentous journey. Behind them come Jerry, with a heart overflowing with happiness because she was Marjorie's maid of honor.

Marjorie followed Jerry, her lovely face wearing the mildly serious expression which came to her naturally in moments of deep reverence. She was so utterly beautiful in her brave white array that Hal, watching her with his heart in his eyes as she came drifting toward him, was convinced that he could never hope to be truly worthy of her. Ronny followed with the ring on a white velvet pillow, and the flower girls came last.

From the balcony came the tenderest of all love songs, "Oh, Promise Me." The singers had begun the singing of it before the appearance of the bridal party. As the little procession began to move down the long aisle toward the white violet smothered altar, the exquisite third verse of the song which is seldom sung floated out upon the roomful of rapt spectators.

Oh, promise me that when with bated breath
I wait the presence of the angel Death,
You will be near me, guide my faltering feet,
And softly breathe these words in accents sweet.
Come sometime to me from that distant shore
Caress and comfort as in days of yore;
Triumphant over death our life shall be:
Oh, promise me; oh, promise me.

Back on the wall behind the altar a blue-eyed man looked down from a portrait with the same kindly, questioning expression Marjorie had always read in his fine eyes. She had asked that the study portrait might be brought down and hung on the wall behind the altar. "I should like him to be there," she had said simply to Miss Susanna. The old lady had replied rather huskily: "I am sure he will be."

When within a few feet of the flower-decked spot where Hal and his best man, Danny Seabrooke, waited for her, she cast a calm friendly glance upward at Brooke Hamilton's portrait. She thought she could almost catch a gleam of approval in his eyes. Then her eyes wandered to Hal, and she smiled and blushed in a kind of tender confusion.

The wedding party took their places before the altar. At Marjorie's request Mrs. Dean joined her husband and daughter there. Marjorie had declared that she could not be content not to have both her superior officers beside her at the great moment.

Came the solemn, beautiful words of the Episcopal ring service. Marjorie loved the deep tones of Hal's voice as he made his vows to her of life and death. Her own replies came clear and steady. She had found love and was happily confident for the future. Then their vows were plighted and Hal had placed the ring of their covenant upon her finger.

"Sweetheart," he said, as he kissed the little ringed hand and then sought her lips. Then he whispered with the fondness of proud possession: "Marjorie Dean Macy."

THE END.

Lightning Source UK Ltd.
Milton Keynes UK
UKHW010945281222
414514UK00004B/174